A WITCH AND A HARD PLACE

A WITCH AND A HARD PLACE

THE WITCH NEXT DOOR™ BOOK SEVEN

JUDITH BERENS

LMBPN Publishing
PMB 196, 2540 South Maryland Pkwy
Las Vegas, NV 89109

First US edition, December 2019
Version 1.02, December 2020
ebook ISBN: 978-1-64202-664-1
Print ISBN: 978-1-64202-665-8

THE WITCH AND A HARD PLACE TEAM

Thanks to the JIT Readers

Kathleen Fettig
Diane L. Smith
Peter Manis
Jeff Eaton
Debi Sateren
Dorothy Lloyd
Deb Mader
Jeff Goode
Dave Hicks
Larry Omans

If we've missed anyone, please let us know!

Editor
SkyHunter Editing Team

DEDICATIONS

From Martha

To everyone who still believes in magic
and all the possibilities that holds.
To all the readers who make this
entire ride so much fun.
And to my son, Louie and so many wonderful friends who
remind me all the time of what
really matters and how wonderful
life can be in any given moment.

From Michael

To Family, Friends and
Those Who Love
To Read.
May We All Enjoy Grace
To Live The Life We Are
Called.

ONE

Roads through the Sahara Desert were few and far between. Most of the single main highway that stretched from the northern coast of Libya down through the rolling dunes and sunbaked wastelands that sprawled ever southward was unpaved too. The other roads, traversed at one's peril, didn't officially have names out there amidst the sea of sand.

"It's very easy to get lost if you don't know where you're going." Magnus Ungert gripped the steering wheel of his Jeep Wrangler and barreled down one such unnamed road in the wasteland. "Carmichael knew what he was doing when he set up shop in the world's dead zone." The hybrid warlock glanced at the black-and-silver pin he'd stuck through his thick canvas jacket below the collar. Right now, that jacket lay in the passenger seat beside him, thrown off in the evening heat the night before when he had stopped to refuel before setting out into the middle of nowhere.

He reached reflexively for the jacket and the pin that winked at him in an invitation, then thought better of it. "I already know where I'm going. And if it keeps those idiots from getting any closer to the High Seat, the network can wait." He shook his head and blinked at the poorly packed dirt and sand of the road through the Fezzan region that both cut through the desert and was simultaneously swallowed by it. He'd passed Zillah not that long before—one of the last oasis towns for a very long distance—without stopping. "Carmichael sent out the call and the rest of us come running, don't we?" He snorted and pounded a hand on the steering wheel. His vehicle flurried a constant spout of dust and sand behind him in as much of a straight line as anyone ever made out there. "He said we're close. If he's wrong, I'll—"

With a grunt of surprise, he frowned and narrowed his eyes at the desert road. Warily, he leaned forward to squint into the semi-darkness of the murky light before sunrise. It was early enough that he wasn't blinded by the sun soon to rise ahead, but there was enough darkness to make him doubt what he saw silhouetted against the gray-blue light. "What the hell is that?"

A long, rectangular shape grew by the second, standing off the road ahead of him. He pumped the brakes to avoid skidding over the sand as he slowed from doing a little over ninety. The warlock's eyes widened and he chuckled.

"That's them. Right there waiting for me, like a five-course dinner on the table. Ha!" His hand thumped on the steering wheel again, and he pulled the Jeep to a stop about a dozen yards behind what was now clearly a Winnebago Adventurer.

The lights of the RV were off, and from where he had stopped, Magnus couldn't hear any movement or generators or any noise at all. The only sound was the cool desert air as it whispered across the sand, which would soon be too hot for his liking. "This has to be the witch everyone's looking for." He turned off the vehicle, sniffed, and sneered through the windshield. "This is too easy."

Cautiously and quietly, he opened the door and he left it open so he wouldn't alert that stupid witch and her annoying werewolf to his presence. If they were still asleep, all the better. With slow steps, the warlock moved down the dirt road between the rising dunes on either side and flexed his fingers at his sides. A gust of wind picked up to pelt the back of the RV with sand and a few larger pebbles from the dirt road. He stepped around to the right side of the Winnebago, knowing he'd find an entrance there that would give him easier access and hopefully the advantage of surprise against the occupants—something he wouldn't have if he tried to climb through the front door.

When he rounded the back of the vehicle, he stopped.

A faded blue beach towel was spread out in the sand beside the vehicle, slowly being covered by the winds and the ever-shifting desert. On that towel, though, was Lily Antony herself. The young witch lay on her back in a zip-up hoodie and baggy sweatpants, her arms resting serenely at her sides. Her blonde hair fanned out around her head, some of it completely covered by the sand that had drifted toward her for however long she'd been lying here.

Magnus smirked. *I heard she was dumb, but how stupid does someone have to be to sleep on the side of the road in the Sahara without shelter? Unarmed?* It took considerable willpower not to snort at how easy a catch this would be. Carmichael had mentioned rewards for any members of the Black Heron Society who personally delivered this sleeping witch to the High Seat. *It looks like that's gonna be me.*

The warlock's feet made no noise over the loose sand as he moved toward the witch. When he stopped only a yard away, he stretched his fingers again. Red, shimmering orbs of a containment spell flared to life in his palms and he couldn't wait to use them.

As he raised a hand toward her, Lily's eyes flew open. They glowed a bright, blazing white in the twilight before dawn.

"What the—" He didn't see the long copper rod in the young witch's hand until the inverted U shape at its tip raised and pointed directly at him. The same white beam of light burst from the tip of the rod and struck him squarely in the chest. Before he could scream, he was gone, erased from the desert as if he'd never been there.

Lily raised her head off the towel and stared at where the warlock had stood in front of her. After a moment, she lowered her head onto the towel again and sighed. "I don't care how quiet he was. I wasn't done meditating." She glanced at the copper rod of the Varelos in her hand. "And now that conversation's over. Thanks for the heads-up, though."

She pushed herself up until she sat on the towel and

gazed west down the road through Fezzan. "Huh. I honestly didn't expect them to drive after us now that we're this close. Let's go see what he left us."

With a regretful sigh—she really had enjoyed the meditation time—she pushed quickly to her feet and moved down the road toward the warlock's abandoned Jeep. The driver-side door was still open. The copper Varelos rod swung in her hand. When she reached the vehicle, she climbed inside, sat firmly in the driver's seat, and glanced around. "It looks like a car that can make it across the Sahara," she mused and flipped the visor down to check for anything tucked behind it but found nothing. "I'd still take the Winnie over this any day. Oh, hey... Look at that."

After a moment's hesitation, she picked up the warlock's canvas jacket, careful not to let her fingers touch the black-and-silver pin beneath the collar with the image she knew only too well—a black heron, its wings outstretched in flight and neck slightly bent in the telltale U shape. "Well, at least I didn't teleport a random Warlock ready to blast me to oblivion. Now, I have proof of who he was working for." With a shrug, she dropped the jacket onto the passenger seat and focused on the phone in the center console.

It was locked, of course, when she picked it up. But days of not being able to sleep—thanks to the blaze of yellow light only she could see that lit the way toward her mom with no off switch—had given her an abundance of time to practice her most powerful spells. Which was another advantage, as those were really the only kinds an Optatus witch needed.

"I can't believe it took me this long to try spells on electronics." She tapped the smartphone's screen, which buzzed with a few static lines for a second before it unlocked and took her immediately to the home screen. She opened the text messages, scanned them quickly, and uttered a wry chuckle. "Oh, man. These people really are having a hard time, aren't they?" Another quick glance around the Jeep showed her only a few half-empty bottles of water, a sleeping bag, an open suitcase only partially filled with clothes, and nothing else besides. "I wonder if—"

"Lily?" Romeo's voice was faint, swept away by the winds through the sand despite how loudly he'd shouted.

The young witch leaned toward the open door and glanced at the phone again and the text that could possibly have gone to every Black Heron member. "Yeah?"

He bounded out of the Winnie and jogged toward the Jeep. "Did you actually steal someone's car?"

Lily tapped the copper Varelos rod against her shoulder and stared blankly at the steering wheel. "Well, not yet."

TWO

"Okay, Lil. I know 'yet' is the operative word, here." Romeo stopped beside the Jeep's open door and propped himself up on the doorframe. "But let's not follow that all the way through, okay?"

Lily turned to look at him with a smirk. "Is it really stealing if the owner simply left it?"

He studied the mischievous curve of her lips, the dark circles of sleeplessness under her eyes, and the foggy glaze that had been her constant expression for the last two days. "It depends on what actually happened to the owner."

She rolled her eyes. "He tried to sneak up on me. I was meditating, and this trusty artifact told me he was standing right there over me." She lifted the Varelos a little before she turned to meet his gaze. "I only wanted him to go away."

"Wait, what? Why didn't you wake me?" He sent the copper rod a wary look. "You know I would've helped you."

"I know. But I didn't need you to. I only…" She sighed and gave a half-hearted shrug. "I only thought about the guy leaving me alone and then he was gone."

"Because of that thing." He nodded at the Varelos.

"I guess. It turns out the most powerful magical weapon in the world is also an excellent watchdog and problem-solver."

"Lily."

"Yeah."

"What'd you do to the warlock?"

She shrugged again. "Teleported him, probably. I have no idea where, but that's not really the most important thing right now, is it?"

"No, I'd say the most important thing is that you actually teleported a random magical without knowing who he was or what he wanted."

"Romeo, he wanted to attack me. He had spells ready and everything. He's a Black Heron member."

"It's kinda hard to be sure about that when the guy's not around to ask, isn't it?"

Lily snatched the canvas jacket on the passenger seat beside her and lifted the collar. "I'm fairly sure this says enough."

He scowled at the black-and-silver heron pin, then shook his head. "You didn't know that before he disappeared."

"But the Varelos did." She lifted the warlock's phone from her lap, held it out toward him, and nodded. "Go ahead and read it."

Romeo chewed on the inside of his cheek and studied

her intently before he finally took the stranger's phone and read the text aloud. "'The prodigal hybrids are out of control, and it's become quite clear that they're acting against the interests of the High Seat and our organization as a whole. Any of you still loyal to the cause are to now engage our wayward associates as enemies until the final preparations have been made and the Transference is complete.'" He held the phone out to her with a scowl. "These people are nuts."

"Right." She took the phone and dropped it back in the cupholder. "And apparently, they have far more problems now than simply pursuing us. Which is a good thing, for the most part."

"Or it merely makes them much more dangerous than they already were."

She laughed and looked at him with wide, amused eyes. "You're kinda being a drag this morning."

He shook his head. "I'm being realistic, Lil. Do you think maybe four days with no sleep is starting to get to you?"

"Probably." Lily slid out of the driver's seat, and he stepped back to give her space. She shut the door behind her and lifted the Varelos to settle it against her shoulder. "I don't feel so tired or crazy with this thing, though."

"I've noticed." The werewolf followed her down the road toward the Winnie again. "Maybe it's a good idea to let go of it for a little while. You know, put it somewhere safe and try to get some rest that doesn't involve so much...meditating."

She sent him a coy glance over her shoulder. "This

thing is the only way I've been able to get any rest at all. I know you can't see this light stretching from me and forever across the desert toward the next place we're supposed to be. You'll have to believe me when I say it's impossible to sleep or relax or ignore this...beacon, except for when I sit down for a little chat with this." The Varelos tapped against her shoulder. "It drowns everything else out."

Romeo sighed and held the Winnie's side door open for her as she climbed the two steps inside. "Okay, Lil. Can we settle on a compromise, then?"

Lily slumped onto the couch, crossed one leg over the other, and settled the copper rod over her lap. "It depends on what it is."

"When we get where we're supposed to go and that light disappears, you put that thing away. I'll put it up in the cabinet—or somewhere you can't find it if you want." Slowly, he lowered himself onto the couch beside her and tried not to stare at the copper rod that had been in her hand for at least the last forty-eight hours. "If the beacon I can't see is gone, you won't need your fancy meditation rod to rest, right?"

She licked her lips and stared at the magical artifact she'd taken from the god of dreams in Greece and pretended to hand over to the Vátran Royal while they crossed the Mediterranean in half an hour. "I'm sorry," she whispered.

"For what?"

"I know you don't like it." She looked at him and leaned back against the couch. "I know I've been hanging onto it—too much, probably. But it's kind of the only life-line I have right now. Besides you." A wry chuckle escaped her. "Trust me, if you had the ability to make this nonstop-shining light go away so I could actually sleep, I wouldn't carry this around."

He smirked. "You know, we haven't tried everything." He tucked a few strands of her blonde, sand-dusted hair behind her ear, and she chuckled when even more grains spilled down the front of her hoodie. When he kissed her, he felt her relax a little more and pulled her up onto his lap until she straddled him on the couch. "A different kinda magic," he muttered against her lips.

Lily released a huge sigh. "We should get going."

His fingers slipped under the hem of her hoodie and trailed up across her back. "We have five minutes." She laughed and slipped her arms up over his shoulders to play with the dark curls at the back of his neck. His green eyes flecked with gold shimmered in her vision—not from magical interference or even tears but because it had become hard to see straight. He wiggled his eyebrows. "A very exhausting five minutes."

With another sigh, she pressed her forehead against his. "It won't work."

"You don't know that."

"I do."

"Well, you're gonna have to forgive me if I don't take your word for it." He kissed her again, stood from the couch with her in his arms, and felt her legs tighten around him. "We might as well take advantage of the time between a warlock attack before sunrise and the next magical who wants to try to capture us. Again."

She chuckled. "So shouldn't we be driving and following the light—"

"Stop talking." He stared at her as he carried her through the Winnie's short hallway into the bedroom in the back.

The young witch bit her lip and couldn't look away from his eyes. She kissed him instead and didn't say another word. *There won't be much time for this anyway when we get to wherever this stupid light is leading us. Enjoy it, Lily.*

THREE

Lily nursed her cup of coffee in the passenger seat of the Winnebago, the Varelos rod settled across her lap. Behind the wheel, Romeo took a deep breath and smirked at the desert that stretched all around them in every direction. "What are you smiling about now?" she asked and took another sip.

He didn't look at her, although it wouldn't have been an issue with literally nothing on the barely visible road and no real obstacles to avoid. "The same thing as the last time you asked."

"That was half an hour ago."

"I know."

The morning sunlight illuminated his lips, chin, and the angle of his jaw with the rest of his face cast in shadow by the visor as they drove toward the sun. Shaking her head, Lily glanced out her window to see the bright-yellow line of glowing energy cut across the desert, always stretching from her to what she hoped was really their final destination. "When we get there," she said, focused on the beacon only she could see, "when we're at the place in my vision, you know you can't come with me, right?"

"What?"

"The Black Heron's waiting for me. They want me to 'complete the circle' for their final spell. If you come with me, you'll be simply another werewolf they can use."

"Stop—"

She swallowed. "They'll torture you like all the other magicals they kidnapped, Romeo. And they'll try to take your magic too and use it for the transference spell. I can't let that happen. When we get to that wall of orange light, wherever we're going, I want you to stay with the Winnie. Or take it somewhere else—"

Romeo slammed his foot down on the brake and the Winnie slid to a jerky stop on the dirt road. He thrust the gear into park and sat there, white-knuckling the steering wheel and glaring out the windshield. His jaw flexed repeatedly and his chest heaved.

"I couldn't have come this far without you," she added and finally turned to look at him. "We both know that. But I can't let you walk in there with me because we also both know exactly what they'll do to you. I won't let you—"

"You don't get to let me do anything." He took a breath and turned to look at her. "I'm all for your plan, Lil. You won't tell me what it is, which is fine because I trust you. You know what you're doing. But if walking into that place by yourself—without me—is part of that plan, we need to come up with a new one."

"Romeo—"

"Don't." His nostrils flared and a flush rose high on his cheeks and the tips of his ears. "I won't sit this one out."

"They'll hurt you."

"They'll hurt you, Lil." He shook his head. "You already expect that."

"But I can handle it."

"So can I."

Lily tilted her head and frowned. "I don't like pulling the type-of-magic card, especially with you, but there's only one Optatus witch in this RV."

Romeo raised his eyebrows and pinned her with a piercing gaze. "Then she'd better come up with a way for the other guy to handle whatever the Black Heron can throw at him." She opened her mouth to protest again, but he shook his head. "I swear, Lily, if you tell me to stay behind, I'll tie you to the bed and leave you there. Then, I'll use that creepy metal stick myself and make you take me with you."

Her mouth dropped open and she stared at him in real surprise. "That's actually a very effective threat."

"It's not a threat, Lil." He set his hand on the center console, palm up, and waited for her to lace her fingers through his. "I won't give up on you or this thing we're doing. Whatever comes next—getting your mom out of there and keeping those wackjobs from ruining magic for everyone—I'm in it with you. You might be an Optatus witch, but I'm much faster than you on four legs."

After she'd searched his gaze for a few seconds, she squeezed his hand. "That'd be a good match. Us fighting each other."

"Not as good as us fighting together." He lowered his head toward her and clenched his jaw. "Promise me you won't go in there by yourself. I'm talkin' no loopholes and no tricks. You can't simply step out in the middle of the night while I'm asleep and disappear, got it?"

"Yeah."

"Say it."

"I promise."

Romeo took a deep breath and visible relief flooded over him as he straightened in the driver's seat and rubbed his thumb over the back of her hand. "Okay."

"You know that means I'm gonna have to use the Varelos for more than only meditating, then, right?"

"Yeah, I assumed that was part of the process."

Lily nodded. "New plan, then. Are you sure you really want to go in there with me?"

He squeezed her hand, pulled his fingers gently away from hers, and flipped the gearshift back into drive. "Don't ask me that again, okay?"

"Okay."

The Winnie accelerated slowly down the barely visible road, and they were back to their normal speed in under a minute. He shook his head and huffed out a strained chuckle. "You know, when I imagined threatening to tie you to the bed, it was under completely different circumstances."

She snorted. "Well, you don't have to rule that out completely. Let's finish this first."

"So you're sayin' you'd be into it?" He turned his head a little to shoot her a sideways glance.

"You'd like that, wouldn't you?"

Romeo chuckled, and the tension between them diffused—at least as much as it could, considering where they were headed and what they'd face when they got there.

Five minutes later, she stared with tired, burning eyes at the bright beacon of yellow magic that always pointed them in the right direction. *Oh, look. It's moving. Huh. I guess I'm hallucinating.* She focused out her window but had to turn her head a little to follow the yellow glow that didn't move diagonally to the southeast anymore but almost completely south. "Oh, wait!"

"What?" Romeo glanced quickly at her, then searched the empty dunes and wind-gusted sand around the Winnie.

"It's moving—that way. We need to go straight that way!" She jabbed her finger at the window.

"Lily, I don't—"

"The light, Romeo. We have to get off the road."

"Oh." He slowed and turned left, navigating carefully over the sand that really wasn't meant for off-roading in an RV. "So it's another straight line, huh?"

"Yeah." This time, she pointed directly in front of them through the windshield. "Right in front of us. Keep going straight."

The Winnie fell silent for a few minutes before he cleared his throat. "So, there's definitely a part of me that's totally down to drive through the middle of nowhere without any roads at all."

When he didn't follow that up with what she knew

was the other side of that particular coin, she leaned forward and spread her arms. "And the other part of you?"

"Um... The other part of me knows that we're headed toward the middle of nowhere in the Sahara without any roads at all."

"We'll be fine." Lily couldn't stop staring at the horizon in front of them, broken only by the mountains of sand in every direction. Romeo had to move the Winnie slowly around a particularly large dune that was too big for them to climb. *And they're only gonna get bigger.* "Yeah, we'll be fine, but keep following the light."

"I'm gonna need you to keep me updated on that."

"I will." She leaned forward in the passenger seat and searched the desert for anything that might look remotely like the end of their journey. So far, it was only that blazing yellow beacon leading the way as it seared through the windshield and all the empty sand in front of them for much farther than she could see.

"You think we'll run into another John out here?" he asked.

"Another John?"

"The wandering spirit who took us to the Nile and filled our gas."

When she looked at him, he was smiling, although it seemed a little tight. "I have no idea. But it wouldn't surprise me at all if we ended up meeting someone else out here." *Especially since we're so close to the end. I'm sure of it this time.*

FOUR

L ily clutched the Varelos in her hands while the sound of her deep breathing echoed in her head. White light surrounded her and the soft, buzzing tingle of the copper rod pulsed from her hands and up her arms.

What can I do to protect him?

The Varelos' echoing, multi-toned voice greeted her instantly. *"You must make him vulnerable."*

I'll already do that by bringing Romeo with me into that place when we get there—whatever it is. I need a spell.

"You have a spell. The amulet around your neck will do what you wish to save him. But if you use it, you will not save your mother."

She sighed. *Okay, we've been at these conversations for days, now. Don't you think it's about time you cut out the riddles and give it to me straight?*

"Riddles or not, that is not your issue."

Oh, good. You're a shrink now too, huh?

"If you wish to protect Romeo, the power of your amulet must be used twice. Once within him and once by him."

By him? He's a werewolf. Romeo can't cast the reversal spell even if he wanted to.

"Only if what he is never changes. It will come from within and without. And you must be the one to put it there each time."

Her breath quickened a little when the pieces came together. I do actually need him for this whole thing, don't I?

"If you want what you desire, yes."

Then show me the spell that will help him.

A blast of images filtered through Lily's mind all at once—the reversal spell she would have to bind to Romeo, the things he'd have to endure at the hands of the Black Heron society, the possibility of him believing everything she said once the Black Heron had them instead of trusting to what she had to tell him now before they reached the end.

Is this a vision of the future?

"A possible future. I do not prophesy, witch. I merely deliver what you seek."

She couldn't think of anything else to say, so she severed the connection with the Varelos. The tingling in her arms and hands faded, the white light surrounding her disappeared, and the glare of the yellow beacon lit up behind her eyelids again. Lily opened her eyes and stared at the straight yellow line in front of them, which cut past a massive dune rising on their left.

"Are you okay?" Romeo glanced at her as the Winnie bumped over the constantly shifting sands.

"Yeah." She set the artifact across her lap again and rubbed her face. "I discovered how we can do this together. How to keep you safe."

"Wow." He grinned. "That only took you forty minutes."

"What?" She glanced at the clock on the dashboard. "That went fast."

"I bet it does when you're plugged into that thing like a virtual reality game." When she didn't respond or even smile, he slowed the vehicle so he could look at her for longer than a few seconds. "What's wrong?"

She licked her lips, straightened in the passenger seat, and nodded. "Okay. I have to tell you something, and I can't explain it completely or it won't work."

"A secret plan, huh? It doesn't involve leaving me behind at all, does it?"

"No." Finally, she did smile but only a little. "You're definitely coming with me. And you might be getting more than you bargained for."

"Not with you." He nodded at her to continue. "I can handle it, Lil."

"When we get to where they're holding my mom, we have to let them—"

The Winnie jostled a little, stopped, and tilted a few degrees to the side. "Crap." Romeo pumped the gas pedal, revved the engine, and even from inside with the windows rolled up, they could hear the free spin of at least one of the tires and the spray of sand knock up against the under-carriage.

"Are we stuck?" Lily glanced at the side mirror but couldn't see anything but sand and more sand.

"Yeah, that's what it feels like. I knew this was gonna happen."

"Really?" She smirked at him and unbuckled her seat-belt. "At least one of us was thinking about it. I should've whipped up some shields for the tires or something before we left the road."

"You had enough on your mind." He unbuckled his seatbelt, stood, and headed toward the side door.

"I still do." She followed him once she'd set the Varelos gently in the passenger seat. "It doesn't mean my magic's broken."

"Let's go check, then." When he opened the side door, the drop to the sand seemed much lower than normal. "Oh, yeah. This is awesome." He stepped back from the vehicle and gestured at both tires on the passenger side. "Two wheels stuck in the sand."

"It's an easy fix." She rolled her shoulders and flexed her hands. "Exactly like when I got out to push the other day, remember?"

"Yeah, I remember. For pushing an RV through the desert, you didn't sweat nearly as much as I thought you would."

"I wish I could say the same about you." She winked at him and cast a small, gentle force spell against the Winnie's side. The RV rocked in the sand and didn't do much else. "Huh. It's really stuck." She cast again and flicking her fingers for the invisible spark that jostled the RV and rocked it wildly. Unfortunately, it didn't come up nearly as much as they needed it to. "Is there quicksand in the desert?"

Romeo raised his eyebrows. "Probably. I haven't spent that much time in the Sahara before this, so..."

"Okay, so we simply need to keep going." Lily frowned at the side of the Winnebago that had been their home for the last three months and almost halfway across the world. The tires glinted at her in the sun and seemed to vibrate in her vision. She clenched her eyes shut, shook her head, and tried again.

"Are you okay?"

"Yep. Everything's a little...wiggly, is all."

He sighed. "I'll go push."

"No. I got this."

"You're swaying on your feet, Lil."

She stepped her legs a little farther apart for better support. "There. See? Steady as a rock."

"Seriously, I can push."

"And I can still cast spells that actually help us." Lily clapped and summoned her Optatus magic. The black cloud bloomed between her palms to crackled and churn and block out the sunlight.

"Hey, don't run yourself into the ground."

"I'm fine." She flicked her palms toward the RV and raised her arms. Two streaks of her Optatus magic flashed from her hands, buzzed around the tires, and lifted them out of the sand trap with a loud hiss of falling sand. "See?" She smirked at him, and the RV continued to raise on its side until it now tilted farther than it should have toward the driver's side. "We're good."

"Careful—" Romeo pressed his lips together.

"I *am* careful—"

"You're gonna tip it over!"

Lily whipped her head toward the RV and jerked her hands to her sides again. The Winnie rocked toward them, and the right-hand tires sank into the sand again, even deeper than before. The bottom of the side door was now mere inches from the ground. "Oh, boy."

"Okay." Romeo scratched the back of his head and cast her a sidelong glance. "I'll push."

"Yeah..." She bit her lip and glanced at her hands. *I could do this if I could sleep.* "Do you want me to help from back there?"

"Nope. I got it." He'd almost reached the back of the Winnie when the wind kicked up and sprayed the top layer of sand from the dune beside him. He turned his back to the wind, covered his eyes, and paused. "Hey..." After a hasty sniff of the air, he crouched and moved quickly toward her. "Get down."

"What?"

"Get down. Someone's coming."

"How do you—"

"I can smell it. Just...wait."

They hunkered against the side of the Winnebago for a few minutes, but nothing happened. Lily gazed out across the desert. "Do you think you maybe picked up something else?"

Romeo gave her an exasperated glance. "I trust my

nose more than I trust your magic right now."

"Wow. Okay."

"I mean...sorry." He lowered his voice. "I didn't mean it like that. I only—" He sniffed again and a low growl escaped his throat. His eyes flashed the bright silver as they did before a shift, and he placed a hand on her shoulder. "Stay here."

"No, thanks. The whole 'don't tell me to stay behind' thing works both ways, you know."

He took another deep sniff of the hot, dry air and scowled. "What is that?"

Right on cue, the ground trembled beneath them and the vehicle sank a little lower into the sand. Something that sounded like a cross between a wild boar and a grunting bear rose from the other side of the RV and the huge dune beside them. They glanced at each other. She had to steady herself against the rumble across the ground again, and he grasped her arm in support. More sand shivered from the top of the dune to fill the space between it and the Winnebago. The grunting sound repeated, much louder this time, and two massive forms emerged from behind the dune in front of the RV.

Lily gaped and shook her head. "Please tell me I'm not hallucinating right now."

"If you are, so am I." He stared at the figures that appeared in front of them. "Is that a camel?"

"I think so." She held his arm even tighter. "I don't think the ground's supposed to shake like this with only two of them."

"I think you're right."

FIVE

The first camel stopped and the loops on its bridle jingled as its rider pulled it up short in front of the Winnebago. The rider was covered from head to toe in light-colored cloth wound around his arms and legs, torso, neck, and head so only his bright green eyes were visible. The camel and rider who'd come up behind him moved on and the second rider cast the vehicle and its passengers a brief glance before he gazed ahead again toward the west.

In the next moment, the second camel blinked out of existence and three more appeared behind it. The animals moved slowly on long legs and uttered the odd, guttural grunts and chuffs, and every rider swayed from side to side with the processional gait. One by one, they disappeared.

"Does this make you think of the mountains in Mexico?" Romeo muttered.

"And teleporting caravans? Yeah. Only mountains made of sand this time." Lily tried to hold the gaze of the first rider who'd broken off from the camel parade as the ground vibrated beneath her. "Do you think it was the camels you smelled?"

He barely shook his head. "Okay, they definitely smell. But I meant the rider."

"Oh, good. Another magical race we get to meet for the first time." She closed her eyes against a gust of sand kicked up by a very large, very dark-haired camel before it vanished and took its rider, three saddlebags, and a sand-colored covered wagon with it.

The first man patted the base of his mount's neck twice, and the animal stepped toward the witch and the werewolf with a low grunt. "It is an unusual way to make your passage." His bright gaze flicked toward the Winnie.

She nodded. "We know. It's all we have, though."

His eyes narrowed above the cloth draped around his face and he turned his head briefly to note all the other camels that continued to vanish on their right. "Perhaps not. Will you join us?"

"It depends on where you're going."

"Lily..."

She nudged Romeo gently with an elbow but didn't look away from the rider. "That's an invitation to help us." He sighed.

"A safe place," the rider replied. "It's not far." He gestured with a hand toward the disappearing animals. "Not nearly as far as you have still to go."

She glanced at the werewolf and whispered, "Do you think he actually knows where we're headed?"

"Come on. Our RV's stuck in the middle of the desert. Of course we have a long way to go."

The rider tilted his head and studied her. "Perhaps a gift for the Optatus will help you make your decision."

"Lily, how come everyone we meet suddenly knows what you are?"

"Probably because I do too now." She glanced at him. "This might be our next John the wandering spirit. And it's rude to turn gifts down, right?"

"You simply can't say no, can you?"

Behind the rider, the procession continued to emerge from behind the huge dune. Camel after camel and wagon after wagon disappeared once they passed the man who was most likely some kind of leader. With a small, concise nod at the first rider, Lily smiled. "We'll join you. Thank you."

Romeo chewed on the inside of his cheek and closed his eyes.

The stranger nodded. "Come. Be sure to walk beside Ahara."

Leaning down toward Lily's ear, the werewolf muttered, "That's the camel, right?"

"It's probably a good guess."

They stepped beside the camel, who grunted but didn't pull on its reins to so much as acknowledge them with a glance. The rider didn't look at them either and together, they filled the gap in the procession and walked toward the place where everyone vanished.

She gasped at the cold tingle that rushed across her limbs and stared in disbelief. They stood at the edge of a village. Some of the huts wavered in and out of her vision amidst huge palm, date, and fig trees, verdant ferns and bushes, a stone well, and a massive pond in the very center of it all. When she turned, the air behind them shimmered like the mirage she'd expected to see in the desert. There was the Winnie, wavering a little and still quite clearly stuck in the sand.

"Come." The first rider and his camel were a few yards ahead of them now and the man clicked his tongue. The animal bent its knees and lowered itself to the soil and the few blades of grass that grew in the hidden oasis. With a quick, graceful swing of his leg, the stranger dismounted and stepped toward his awestruck guests as he pulled the cloth slowly from his head and down from over his face. He greeted them with a calm, amused smile and pulled off one glove before he extended a hand. "Welcome."

"Thank you." Lily shook his hand, surprised by the confusing feeling of both a firm grip and what felt like nothing more than warm air against her fingers at the same time.

"You may call me Marwan."

"Lily."

"Romeo." He shook their host's extended hand as well and his brows flickered together quickly when he felt the same strange sensation.

"Well met, my friends." Marwan dragged the cloth back even farther from his head and shook out a few long, pitch-black curls that most likely hung far below his shoulders. "Do either of you care for a drink?"

Lily glanced at her friend, who'd tilted his head and still stared at his hand. "Please." She nodded to the man and studied his dark hair, tanned skin, and green eyes. *If I didn't know better, I'd say he and Romeo could've been related somehow.* The thought startled her a little.

"This way." He passed his camel, who still lay on the sparse grass in the ring outside the lushest part of the oasis. While he gave her neck a quick, soothing stroke, he muttered something they couldn't hear. The animal grunted and lowered her head to rip a chunk of grass from the earth with her teeth. The man chuckled and turned to wave them forward. "This place has much to give. You two are fortunate to have stopped when and where you did."

"It wasn't planned." Romeo scratched the back of his head. "We got stuck."

"Perhaps." Marwan stopped at a stone well set between two of the huts. Clay cups lined the edge, and he dipped three of them into the cool, clear water before handing one to each of his guests and cradling the last in both hands. "Or perhaps it was on purpose. Merely not your own." A tiny smile flickered at the corner of his mouth. "Drink." When they paused only briefly, he lifted the cup to his own lips and took a long draught.

The young witch and her werewolf companion did the same. It felt like drinking ice and filled her with a burst of energy and calm that she hadn't felt in a long time. When she lowered the cup again, she grinned. "It's sweet."

Romeo eyed the cup with a raised eyebrow despite the fact that he'd also drained it completely. "Are you sure this is water?"

"You may call it that if you wish." Their host replaced his cup on the circular stone wall of the well and clasped his hands in front of him. The young couple set theirs beside his.

Lily gazed at the oasis. The camels moved freely between many well-kept huts and the pool glistened beneath the desert sun as huge birds waded through the shallows. Two children laughed a few yards away. One climbed one of the fig trees while the other shouted for him to go higher. Everywhere she looked, the people smiled, conversed, and moved around with an ease that seemed unnatural for having come from the middle of the Sahara. All of them had the same curly black hair, dark skin, and bright-green eyes. "What is this place?"

"Merely one of many along the journey with no name." Marwan bowed his head, muttered something under his breath, and lifted it again to gaze at his guests. "And a nexus of destinies, perhaps."

That sounds promising. I hope. "It's definitely better than standing in the heat trying to get our RV out of the sand."

"I imagine so." The man's lips twitched but didn't quite curve into a smile. "How do you feel?"

She frowned. "Fine. I..." Her eyes widened and she turned again to make sure she could still see the Winnie through the shimmering wall separating the hidden oasis from the unforgiving Sahara. "It's gone."

"What?" Romeo spun but he saw the Winnie there too, tilting slightly toward them where it stood alone against the next gust of wind that sprayed sand all over it. "You're not talking about the RV."

"No." She looked at him and laughed in disbelief.

"The light. The—" She moved her hand from her chest toward the empty air in front of her. "I guess there's an off switch after all."

"You have been given a gift," Marwan said and nodded sagely.

Her smile faded when it dawned on her that the only thing leading her directly to her mother was now gone. "Actually, um..." She took a deep breath. "I appreciate the sentiment, but I need that light. We're...following it—"

He roared with laughter and held both hands against the light-colored cloth that covered him almost from head to toe. The friends shared a wary glance before their host regained his composure and shook his head. She thought she saw his eyes flash a brighter green when he met her gaze again. "That is merely a reprieve, my friend. Your soul-line will return when you are ready to step into your journey once again. For now, I invite you to rest in comfort and safety."

My soul-line? "Oh. Thank you."

"Have you talked at them enough, Marwan?" A middle-aged woman stepped out of one of the huts, wearing the same draped garments as him and boasting the pitch-black curls, dark skin, and green eyes, which narrowed at the man when she approached them. "It is kind of you to welcome guests but all that kindness is undone by using the time that could be better spent."

With a smirk, he eyed the woman but said nothing.

"I am Hamala." The woman pressed her hands together and lowered her head toward her guests.

"Marwan enjoys twisting truths into winding ropes of confusion."

The man chuckled. "If I have succeeded in confusing an Optatus witch cast across our path, my apologies."

"It's okay." Lily met Hamala's gaze, nodded, and smiled a little.

"I'm confused." Romeo looked from one of their hosts to the other.

Hamala regarded him with a small smile and nodded. "Because you do not recognize our people."

He paused. "Yeah, that. And the fact that it feels like you can read my mind."

"Merely a passing scent on the wind." Marwan fluttered his fingers out to the side and laughed when Hamala slapped his arm.

"We are Masafir," the woman said and frowned at her companion. "One of many tribes. We seek answers very much like those the two of you are so close to revealing."

Lily cleared her throat. "You know I'm an Optatus."

"Yes."

"And you know where we're headed?"

The woman tilted her head slowly from side to side. "We know where you will be, Lily. Where you are going is still unclear until you've reached that point in time."

"Uh..." Romeo fought back a chuckle of disbelief, and Lily nudged him covertly with her elbow.

"You're not the first people to tell us that," the young witch said. "I still don't quite know what it means."

Hamala turned to Marwan and shook her head. "Did you at least offer them a drink?"

"Which they gladly accepted." The man licked his lips, clearly holding back another laugh. "And I mentioned what we have for them."

"Without explaining any of it." The woman tsked and set off across the oasis past the hut from which she'd emerged. "Come with me. This man is an impossible guide for those who do not already know the way."

Lily glanced at Marwan, who merely nodded at her, winked, and turned to shout a warning jest at the young boy pelting his friend with ripe figs. She turned to see Hamala waiting for them, then muttered, "We have to go with her, right?"

Romeo stared after Marwan. "What's with the wink?"

"Seriously? All of this in the middle of the desert, a tribe of Masafir who give us magical water and hopefully have something that can help us, and you're tied up about a wink?"

"Yeah."

She snorted. "Why?"

"Because I couldn't feel his hand when I shook it and now, I can't smell these people at all. It's like they don't even exist."

She caught his hand and gave it a little squeeze. "You can feel that, right?"

He turned his head slowly toward her and nodded.

"Good. So we still exist, and as long as that's true, I want to find out what these people know about 'where I will be.' Plus, he said something about a gift."

The werewolf let her pull him across the Oasis toward

Hamala, unable to hold back a smirk. "It looks like you're feeling better."

"It must be the water." She grinned at him and turned to nod at Hamala that they were coming. "I don't know how long it's gonna last, so let me enjoy it, okay?"

SIX

Hamala waited for them outside another hut and held the curtain over the entrance aside with one arm. Her dark curls fluttered in the breeze, and she raised an eyebrow.

"I think that means hurry up," Lily muttered.

"I still don't like it, Lil."

"I know." When they reached the structure, she released Romeo's hand and nodded at the woman. She stepped inside willingly when Hamala nodded in return. *After whatever that water had in it, I'm ready for this so-called gift.*

Her companion, though, paused at the entrance and tried to peer inside.

"After you," Hamala said, her voice low but still with a hint of amusement.

The werewolf eyed her for a second, then glanced inside the surprisingly darkened hut. "What's in there?"

"You may see many things, my friend." The woman smiled. "But I assure you, they are all for the best."

With a tiny frown, he relented and stepped in after Lily. It was pitch-dark inside until the woman lowered the curtain over the doorway. A hundred candles flared to life at once to illuminate a circular room with cold stone floors that was crowded with people.

"Mirrors?" Lily turned this way and that, realizing the people all around her were only reflections of three—her, Romeo, and the Masafir Hamala.

"They show us everything, do they not?" The woman stopped behind her and a little to the side and nodded at the mirror they both stared at together. Romeo's hand brushed up against Lily's, and he clearly didn't bother to hide his frown. "That is what I love about them. We see in a mirror both what we want to see and what we do not. A reflection reveals the truth of things."

His gaze drifted around the mirror in front of them until it settled on the bottom above the stone floor and the reflection of the woman's boots, which wavered in and out of opacity. "So what's the truth about your feet?"

She chuckled. "That would be my truth, yes? The two of you are here to view your own."

Lily turned just a little to glance at him. His scowl deepened, and she knew he wanted to say again that he didn't like this.

"Wait here." Hamala bowed and turned to vanish through the maze of mirrors that couldn't have possibly fit inside a hut this size.

"I know he said they had a gift for you." Romeo folded his arms. "I know you're going to find out what it is. But these people are a little too 'not here' for my liking."

She smirked and felt much more like herself again with her energy restored. "I have a feeling it has something to do with being in the desert—maybe even the Sahara, specifically." She squeezed his arm. "We'll be fine."

"Uh-huh."

A few seconds later, two more Masafir entered the room of mirrors from opposite sides, their dark curls casting hundreds of shadows against the mirrors and backlit by so much candlelight. The man placed a gentle hand on Romeo's shoulder and the werewolf stiffened. "Come."

"Lily..."

"It is safe for her to see her own truth," the man said and his voice echoed against the reflective surfaces. "As it will be safe for you to see yours."

The second Masafir approached Lily and stopped beside her to stare at them both in the mirror with a gentle smile.

"It's okay," she said.

"How do you know?"

"I just...do." She nodded at Romeo, and he stepped reluctantly through the passageway within the mirrors, his expression one of stony suspicion as the man guided him away.

"You have a stronger intuition than most." Beside Lily, the woman bowed her head and gestured toward the mirror in front of them. "This is meant to strengthen that in you, Optatus."

She nodded. "Okay."

The Masifir gestured with her hand in front of them and left a yellow glow in its wake. It brightened before it shrank into a brilliant ball of yellow light and settled into the center of Lily's chest. The young witch looked down but there was no light there—only in her reflection. "This has already been preparing you," the woman said.

"What is it?"

"The thing that has kept you awake for days. That which has forced you to both ignore it and to pay attention."

"The beacon." She shivered and focused on the yellow glare in her reflection. "I still need it, though."

"Yes. But not for much longer. The light will remain inside you, Optatus, as it remains in the one who put it there for you to see."

"You mean my mom?"

Her companion merely nodded. "But while the light within you will remain, you must sacrifice something else in order to reach your goal. It has not been done before, and yet you are the only one who can see it through."

She raised an eyebrow and glanced at the woman's reflection. "You're not gonna tell me what that sacrifice is, are you?"

"You will know it when the time comes. The gift you have come to receive, however, is this." She gestured toward the mirror again, and the image changed slightly.

Lily's newfound energy from the well water faded to be replaced by the dark circles under her eyes and the wild look of a person who still had so much to do and no ability to sleep. "You have already been purifying yourself for what is to come. The days and nights will run together, Optatus. You will find yourself in the same prison, although with less ground to cover. And that is the greatest power you will have over those who seek to take it from you. When they make their attempts, they will not know that you have already been through this before."

With a sigh, she nodded at her reflection. "The gift of knowledge, huh?"

"And a confirmation that you are on the right path. That what you plan to do with your werewolf friend and with yourself is indeed the fastest course to victory."

"Okay. Well, thanks." *And now I have to discover what this sacrifice is. That sounds like the hardest part.*

The Masafir put her hand on Lily's shoulder and turned them both away from the mirror. The candles—however many there were—flickered out and someone else lifted the curtain over the hut's doorway from the outside. She squinted against the bright sun in the oasis, although her refreshed energy from the well remained. When she turned her head, Romeo stepped out of the next hut over. The werewolf blinked rapidly in the bright sunlight and frowned deeply in confusion. He finally saw her standing in front of the hut they'd entered together and headed toward her. The Masafir who'd taken him away simply smiled and moved in the opposite direction.

"This is the hut we went into, right?" Romeo pointed at the small building behind her.

"Yep."

"And I came out of that one."

She eyed the other hut. "It looks like it."

He puffed out a sigh. "I'm ready to leave this place when you are, Lil."

Lily met the gaze of the woman who'd shown her only her own reflection—who'd only given her more riddles when she had hoped for an actual physical gift to help her. The Masifir smiled, nodded, and returned to the hut.

"Yeah, me too. I only..." She turned and tried to find the shimmering entrance to the oasis. "Where did we come in?"

"Are you leaving so soon?" Marwan's sudden appearance made them both jump, and he chuckled. "My apologies."

"Yeah, we still have a long way to go," she replied. "Thank you for the...gifts."

The man nodded sagely and extended an arm. "This way. Your belongings still wait for you."

Together, they followed him across the oasis. They seemed to have gone more than halfway around the pool shaded by trees—which they hadn't moved around before on their way to the hut—by the time they reached the stone well. "If you'd like another drink before you leave, I won't tell anyone."

She couldn't help a small frown. "Is that not allowed?"

Marwan shrugged. "Who knows? The well doesn't belong to me and mine, anyway."

"Well, thank you." He bowed, and as he turned to leave, she stepped toward the well again for another drink.

"Are you sure that's a good idea?" Romeo eyed it warily. "I know it made you feel better…"

"If it lasts a little longer and helps me stay on my game, why not?"

He frowned for a moment and chewed the inside of his cheek. "All right."

Lily dipped one of the clay cups into the cool water, took a deep breath, and drained the whole thing in a few giant gulps. The refreshing energy coursed through her again, the water still sweet and tingling on her tongue. When she turned back to Romeo, he was frowning at her. "What?"

"What was the gift they gave you?"

She stepped toward him so they could talk without being overheard. "Merely more riddles about being an Optatus. And a sacrifice I'd have to make."

"A what?"

"Something that no one's ever done before, but I'm the only one who can. And that I've already been purifying myself."

He snorted. "I assume no one told you what that sacrifice is supposed to be."

"Nope." She studied his face and glanced at the Masafir milling about the oasis. No one paid them any attention, as if the strangers in their midst had already disappeared. "Did you get a gift?"

Slipping his fingers into hers, Romeo leaned away from

the camel rising to its feet beside them. "Let's get back to the Winnie first, huh?"

She jumped when the camel uttered another chuffing grunt. "Yeah, okay." She looked for Marwan and Hamala or anyone she might have been able to wave to and thank, but all the Masafir had gathered on the other side of the oasis. None of them looked at her again.

SEVEN

Lily's skin prickled when they stepped through the wavering air and out of the hidden oasis. She shuddered despite the Saharan heat bearing down on her again. "I wonder if that's what people see when they see mirages."

Romeo cast a skeptical glance at the pocket of air behind them, then shook his head. "I hope not."

"Why?"

"There's something weird about those people, Lil. Whatever they are. I honestly don't know if they were actually trying to help us or only slow us down."

She opened her mouth to ask what he meant by that but her gaze fell on the Winnebago's tires. "Well, we can strike slowing us down off the list of things they wanted."

"What?"

"More mystical help." She pointed at the tires, both of which were unburied. "At least they helped with our little quicksand problem."

"Right." He pressed his lips together and studied them. "Stand back for a second."

Lily frowned at him as he pressed his shoe cautiously into the sand beside the rear tire. "Okay, I get that you don't like them. You couldn't smell them, couldn't feel Marwan's hand, and yeah, they took us into one hut together and out of two separate doorways. But don't you think you're being a little paranoid?"

"No." Satisfied with the hardness of the sand beneath the rear tire, he stalked toward the front tire to test the sand there, too. He wouldn't meet her gaze.

"I don't get it."

"I said I didn't trust them from the beginning. And they didn't really make it any easier when they—" He stopped and glanced past her at the pocket of air they'd stepped through to enter the oasis. Nothing was visible beyond it now, but they both felt the charge in the air after having passed through that veil twice. "Never mind."

Lily stepped toward the Winnie's side door with him and glanced only briefly in the direction in which the RV still pointed. The bright yellow beacon of light leading them directly south now had reappeared in front of her, undimmed and unaffected by her brief hiatus with the Masafir. "Why won't you tell me?"

He had to tug a few times on the side door's handle before it finally opened. A wash of sand spilled out and left a few piles of it still on the bottom step. "After we're inside, okay?" He held the door open for her.

She folded her arms and regarded him sternly. "You keep looking back there like they're gonna come running out after us but you won't actually look at me. What happened in that hut?"

Finally, he did meet her gaze, and his jaw clenched quickly as he coughed. "I'll tell you when we're moving again. Please, can we go?"

She gave him a half-hearted shrug and stepped into the vehicle. He almost slammed the door behind them but he had to open it again to brush the rest of the sand out into the desert before it would close all the way. She was already seated in the passenger seat, buckled up and with her arms folded, when he joined her at the front and slid behind the wheel.

"Still straight ahead?"

Her gaze following the yellow beacon that stretched as far as she could see across and through the rolling dunes ahead of them and nodded. "All the way."

He started the engine, clicked his seatbelt on, and eased his foot onto the gas until he was sure they wouldn't get stuck in a pit of sand again. Despite her impatience, he waited until he'd increased their speed to fifty miles an hour before he said anything else. "Did you actually...see anything?"

Lily squinted at him. "You're gonna have to be a little more specific than that."

"In the mirrors."

"Oh. Um...not that much. I saw this yellow light come back. It was only in my chest, though. And I saw myself looking like myself. The energized Lily and the version of me that hasn't slept for four days and really felt it." When her self-deprecating humor didn't even get a smirk from him, she swallowed uncomfortably. "What did you see?"

"Kind of the same thing." He pressed his lips together and frowned at the desert. "Kind of."

She watched him with wide eyes. If she gave him enough time, he'd eventually spit out the rest.

"And I saw something I wish I hadn't." His knuckles cracked as his grip tightened on the steering wheel.

"That bad, huh?"

He shot her a quick glance and shook his head. "I don't know if it was bad. I don't know if it was good. I only..." A heavy sigh escaped him, and he shook his head impatiently as he struggled to find the words. "We've had our futures told to us before."

"At least twice, yeah."

"And they came true. Both times. But this time? What I saw...Lily, I don't even know how it's possible."

"Are you gonna actually tell me what it was?"

His glance was a little desperate and he looked away quickly and shook his head. "I can't."

"I'm not buying it."

"I'm serious." Romeo ran a hand through his dark curls and scratched his head. "I want to, Lil. I do. But I think that'll only make it worse. Or ruin something, somehow."

She squinted at his profile as they barreled south through the desert. "Okay. So you think telling me will actually make it happen?"

"I have no idea. But I think telling you will make you change your mind."

"About what?"

This time, his head twitched her way but stopped before a full turn like he couldn't look at her again. "About everything. And I don't wanna risk it."

"Does it have to do with my mom?"

"That woman said we only saw our own truths." He grimaced. "I only saw myself, Lily. Not you or your mom. But at this point, I can't exactly say we're not all connected, can I?"

"No." Lily shook her head and stared out at the sunbaked desert and her constant yellow beacon cutting through all of it. "I guess you can't."

"So." He inclined his head toward the Varelos she'd placed in her lap when she returned to the passenger seat. "You make sure that thing does what it needs to do to get me into the Black Heron's headquarters or whatever. Because I'm still coming with you."

She smirked. "I didn't expect that to change."

Finally, he cracked a tiny smile and kept driving.

"I worked it out a while ago, actually."

"What?"

Lily took a deep breath. "What I have to do to keep you safe. That's what I was about to tell you before we got stuck and the Masafir found us."

Romeo cleared his throat. "So what is it?"

A wry chuckle escaped her. "It's kind of ironic that I can't really tell you that either, huh?"

"Did the Masafir tell you that?"

"Not in so many words, I think. She told me I was on the right path, at least. Which I'm fairly sure means I can't tell you exactly how this is gonna work."

With a shrug, he offered her a smile of assent. "I guess it works both ways, then."

"Yeah, maybe. But what I wanted to tell you earlier is that we...well, I guess it's really only me. We have to make the Black Heron think that I've given up."

"Looking for your mom?" He snorted. "So you found a secret passage when you looked into all those mirrors?"

"Not exactly." Lily slid her hand along the length of the Varelos resting on her lap again. "Like what John said too, remember? 'Let them think the night has already come.'"

"Lily, why do I have a feeling you're planning something really, really not awesome?"

"Because it'll keep you safe and because I'll need your help in there. You're the only person I can trust, and once we find my mom and we're in that place, whatever's on the other side of that shimmering wall I saw in my vision... I'll need you to do something you probably won't understand until that moment."

For a few seconds, both sat in silence. "Honestly, I really don't like it that you're starting to talk in riddles too." Romeo swallowed and leaned forward to stare at the sand that passed quickly beneath them. "Especially to me."

"I know." *But the Varelos said I have to make this possible. I have to do this to him so we can get out of there with my mom.* "I'm gonna make them think I've given up. We know we're walking into the most dangerous place for basically everyone right now. And it'd be seriously dumb not to expect the Black Heron to skip the greetings and move directly to the torture part. Especially after how many times I've refused to join them."

"Were those real invitations, though? I began to think those were the mutant society members trying to grab you for more experiments."

"Maybe." She set her hand on the center console and wiggled her fingers like he had done. His hand slid down to take hers in an instant. "The point is, it's not gonna be pretty when we get there. And I want you to know that whatever happens—whatever you hear or see or whatever they tell you—you can't believe it."

"That's already a given, Lil." He squeezed her hand.

"Okay, then I'll come at it this way. Don't believe what I tell you when we get inside."

"What?"

Lily closed her eyes. *I have to give him at least this much warning.* "I don't know what they're gonna do to me, Romeo. To either of us. But the Varelos gave me a spell to use for you—to keep you safe. And whatever happens after that, know that what I'm telling you right now is the truth. That we're in this together. That I'll definitely need your help when it's time to get my mom out of there. And that I love you."

"I love you too." A confused chuckle escaped him. "But you're not making any sense."

"That's okay. But don't forget this part—this moment right now. Got it?"

He scowled for a moment and his grasp on her hand bordered on painful until he realized how hard he was squeezing her. "Yeah. Got it. You can't give me any more clues?"

"Not if this is gonna work. Sorry."

"Okay, then. You know, I don't really feel that much more prepared than I did five minutes ago."

She snorted. "Me neither."

"Well, at least we're still on the same—"

A bright flash of orange light burst directly in front of them. Romeo braked sharply but the light passed through the windshield anyway and burst across both of them and all the way through the RV. Lily felt the static on her skin and saw his hair rise on end like someone had rubbed a balloon over it. She released his hand to grip the Varelos with both of hers, and the Winnie skidded to a stop.

Complete silence surrounded them, cut by the rhythmic ping of what sounded like the RV's engine trying to cool off. His head whipped toward her. "Are you okay?"

"Yeah." She leaned back and loosened the seatbelt that had drawn tight against her chest. "Yeah, I'm fine. You?"

"If we're ignoring the crazy static and the magical light that ripped through us, yeah. I'm good." Romeo looked at the driver seat and studied the inside of the Winnie. "I thought for sure this thing would be ripped apart—"

"Romeo."

"Yeah."

Lily sat ramrod straight, every muscle of her body tense as she stared at what she didn't think she could possibly be seeing. "Look."

He followed her gaze and his mouth dropped open. "That's a road in the middle of the desert."

"Yep."

"And that's a—"

"Yep." She swallowed and unbuckled her seatbelt, unable to tear her gaze from the golden, glowing tree out there amidst so much sand and lack of life. It was mesmerizing, but she had to look away when she climbed out of her seat and headed toward the Winnie's side door.

Romeo watched her, then quickly unbuckled his seatbelt and tossed it against the door. "Are you sure we should—"

"I think we're here." She didn't stop to look at him and felt like she floated through the RV and down the two steps toward the door. "Come on."

EIGHT

"So yes, this is weird." Romeo let the side door shut behind him. "Seriously, a road that goes absolutely nowhere and a glowing tree that looks like someone's bad attempt to start a forest in the middle of the desert. But... Lily, maybe you shouldn't walk right up to it."

"I have to." She glanced at her chest, where the bright-yellow beacon had been shining for days without end, leading her there. "The light, Romeo. It stops at that tree."

"For real?"

"Totally real." She was aware of him behind her—that he'd stopped to stare at the brilliantly illuminated tree only a foot taller than her with thin, strong branches stretching out and up toward the desert sky. Her feet, though, moved across the sand as if she didn't even have a choice. "I can't believe we're actually here."

Before she knew it, she stood in front of the glowing sapling. Waves of fine sand kicked up around her, blown by the hot breeze that rolled across the dunes. Lily stretched a hand toward the closest branch, her eyes wide. "Do you hear that?"

He cleared his throat. "Hear what?"

"That...sound." The closer her outstretched fingers came to the tree's smooth bark—so full of life and vitality out there where there was nothing to sustain it—the louder that inviting chime became. "Like it's calling me."

"I still don't think it's the best idea to touch a glowing magical tree out in the middle of the desert."

"I think it is." Her fingers came down on the branch and her body went rigid under the connection.

Too many images for her to fully absorb flashed through her mind. She saw her mom smiling and nodding as if Greta Antony were telling her she was doing the right thing. The profile of her mom's lips whispered something into the dry desert sand; a dark room with no windows and no doors; a huge black table in the center of a stone chamber, covered with sparkling vials, glistening black stones; the flashing blade of a knife. She saw chains and smoke, grand rooms draped in silks and beds lined with fur. It was impossible to follow the blast of images in the vision from the tree, although she found something that stood out in each of them, lighting up to show her what was really important in all these places.

Then, she saw a man's hand moving in slow motion. It turned a worn, smooth stone over and over, and the stone lit up in a brilliant flash of gold.

The next thing she knew, she was seated in the sand a few feet from the golden tree, breathing heavily. Romeo dropped to the ground beside her. "What happened?"

For a few seconds, she simply stared at the tree. The tiny buds blooming on its branches glinted at her as they caught the sunlight. Quickly, she glanced at her chest to see that the unending beacon that had led her to the tree was gone—for real this time. Finally, she turned slowly to look up at him and smirked. "Would you believe me if I said more visions?"

He snorted and caught her by the wrists to help her back to her feet. "Yeah, I'd believe it. That's basically all you get these days, isn't it?"

"I think that's part of the Optatus package. At least, from one Optatus to another."

His mouth dropped open. "The visions were from your mom."

"Yep." Despite the heat and the sand whipping around them, Lily wondered why her mouth didn't feel drier. "She left the tree here, too."

Romeo's expression shifted from confusion to resignation. "I'll assume the whole Optatus thing explains how she managed to plant and grow a tree in the Sahara while they brought her here against her will."

"Something like that, yeah." Lily ran a hand through her hair and smoothed the wayward strands blowing across her face. "This was her last clue. The beacon leading me here, the tree, and the visions."

"Did they at least tell you what to do next?"

When she turned to face him again, he frowned before she had a chance to say anything. "Not exactly, no. There was so much but mainly a group of images. There's something in there I know I'm supposed to know, but it's not..."

She shook her head and rubbed at the beginning of a headache. "I need a little more time to figure it out."

"Not too much time, though, right?" He placed a gentle hand on the small of her back and studied her. "It's been a few days since you started...uh, being hurt when they hurt your mom too. That doesn't mean they won't try to hurt her again, which means both of you. I'm not trying to be pessimistic or anything, but—"

"No, you're right. We don't have much time." She dusted her hands off and glanced at where they'd parked the Winnie off the road to nowhere. Then, she turned and studied the nothingness of the desert sprawled in front of her. "This is it, though. This is the exact place I saw in the other visions. The same place the Black Heron network showed me." When she caught his dubious glance in her direction, she snorted. "Trust me, I'm sure. The heron coin is locked up in the Winnie anyway, and I definitely don't need to use it again."

"Okay." Romeo nodded and gave a little shrug. "So we're here."

"Yeah. Now I only need to find that orange wall."

"The what?"

Lily stalked away from him across the sand, her hands held out in front of her as she summoned the yellow glow of her revealing spell in both palms. That didn't show her anything. *Of course it wouldn't be this easy.* "I saw this shimmering, orange-brown wall. I'm very sure it was a ward and that we need to get past it. When we do, we'll find my mom and the man who has her."

"The man with the fake eye?" Romeo stayed where he

was, squinted at the air, and looked for the magic field neither of them could see.

"Yeah. I saw him the last time I used the heron coin, remember?"

"Oh, yeah. I remember. The witch who threw you across the Winnie afterward."

She glanced at him over her shoulder with an apologetic smile. "Right." She raised her hands toward where she thought the warded wall should be and clapped. When she drew her hands apart, the pale pink film of her illusion-detecting spell stretched between her palms, growing by the second. "And this is how we find them both."

Totally focused, she put as much intention and force as she could behind releasing the spell. *Show me the wards and I can get through them.* When she'd pulled her hands apart fully, she shoved them forward and put all her weight behind them. Her spell burst from her hands and streaked across the desert, past the dunes surrounding them and the sand that whipped up in tiny storms. She watched it until the pale pink light fizzled and disappeared. Nothing had changed.

"Huh." Romeo folded his arms. "That one always works."

"I know..." Lily tilted her head in thought. "Maybe it needs more juice."

"Okay, but be careful—"

she clapped again and this time, when she drew her hands apart, the black cloud of her Optatus powers built between her palms. The magic churned and rumbled and grew much faster than it had even a few days before. The young witch allowed herself a small smile. *This is definitely getting easier.*

Releasing her black cloud didn't feel nearly as draining as it usually did. The crackling magic burst from her hands and expanded in every direction. She could feel the power of it searching for the orange-brown wall she knew they had to pass—like an itch she couldn't scratch herself. But like her first spell, her Optatus magic faded and blinked out in a few last wisps of black smoke.

"Still nothing?" She gaped at the empty air in front of her. "Right when I learn how to cast this Optatus magic, it stops working." She threw her hands in the air, let them fall to her thighs with a smack, and turned to face Romeo.

He shrugged. "I wish I had an answer for you, Lil."

"Me too." With a deep breath, she stalked past him again, heading for the Winnie. "It's a good thing we have the most powerful magical weapon with all the answers on board with us, huh?"

He opened his mouth to say—one more time—that she had to be careful with how much she used the artifact. Before he could even begin to speak, the Winnie's side door closed behind her with a soft click. "Right. When all else fails, swing the metal stick that's stronger than an Optatus witch. No problem."

The Winnie rocked a little beneath her rapid movement before the side door burst open again and she leapt over the two stairs and onto the sand. The Varelos swung in her hand like a skinny baseball bat. When she lifted it and smacked it down into her other hand, he almost expected her to spit cracked sunflower-seed shells onto the ground before digging the toe of her sneakers into the sand.

The witch moved past him again without a word and stopped on the other side of the tree. She raised the Varelos in one hand and thrust it into the sky. A pink flash emitted from the upside-down U on its tip and all the sharp, glittering tines at the ends. The copper rod's magic did as much as her own, and the elusive orange-brown wards remained exactly that.

Lily sighed. "Okay, fine. We'll have to dig a little deeper to find the answer." She sat on the sand beneath what little shade the golden tree provided in the desert and leaned her back against the narrow trunk. The Varelos settled into both her hands again, and she closed her eyes.

"Lily—"

"I'm gonna have a little chat with this, okay?"

Romeo's shadow passed over her and remained, even when he squatted in front of her and rested his forearms on his knees. "We're right out in the open and apparently on the Black Heron's doorstep if your visions showed you the right thing. Sitting under a glowing golden tree to meditate with that is simply asking for trouble."

She cracked one eye open to see him frowning at her. "The last society member who found us was before the sun even came up this morning. And I'm very sure that was an accident on his part. It was also a quick fix."

"We really shouldn't trust luck and someone else's accidents, though."

"When was the last time we were attacked?" She brushed her hand against the leg of his jeans. "Seriously, though. Besides this morning, the only people who found us were those mutant magicals who chased us off the highway and into the desert, in the first place. And they—" Lily stopped and forced out the memory of all those bodies lying in the sand after what her Optatus magic had done to them. "The tracer on the heron coin has worn off. No one knows we're here."

He glanced at the Winnie and the road. "You don't know that."

"Well, even if someone does know we're here, they obviously have no problem with it. We would've been attacked the minute we got here. And we already know the main part of the Black Heron who want me for their magical free-for-all spell and not for back-room experiments also actually want me here. They're waiting for me. Maybe they know, maybe they don't, but I don't really feel like camping out here and waiting for anyone to come looking for us. We can't stop now."

"I know." Romeo sighed, shook his head, and sat on the sand. "So go ahead and have your little powwow with the world's biggest magical weapon of mass destruction."

She smirked at him, and he gave her a little eye-roll in response. "Don't feel like you can't interrupt if something happens, though."

"What's gonna happen?"

Lily raised her shoulder in a weak shrug, rested her head against the trunk, and wrapped both hands around the Varelos. "It could be anything."

NINE

The electric, buzzing jolt of energy moved from the copper rod's cold, sleek surface and into Lily's fingers, hands, and arms. She'd spent so much time connecting with the Varelos that the bright white light and the silence enveloped her almost before she'd even set the intention to speak to it. Her heartbeat pounded in her ears, completely at odds with her slow, even breathing. Somewhere in the back of her mind, she felt the hot, dry air and the sun beating down on her. Exactly like it had with her exhaustion from not sleeping and the wounds she'd sustained from the Black Heron torturing her mom, though, the Varelos made it all fade away into nothing. Right now, nothing else mattered.

Why can't I find the wards?

"You are not a sworn member of The Black Heron Society," the Varelos replied, hundreds of voices rising in hundreds of tones all at once. *"The desire in their hearts*

opens the gateway you seek. You merely found the entrance by following the light instead of the dark."

You know, I thought I worked that out already. That I followed the beacon my mom left me instead of using the heron coin, right? Lily took a deep breath. *Should I have used the coin instead to get me past those wards?*

"There is no right and wrong in the act of stepping along a path, Optatus. Merely in which path one chooses and where it leads."

Again, you're not being very helpful right now.

"You did not ask for my help."

Forcing herself to stay connected, she attempted a different approach to getting what she wanted. *Okay, then, how can you help me find the wards and get to whatever's next? Where they're keeping my mom?*

"At last. You have finally stumbled upon the only important question. I can help you, witch. And I will if you understand exactly what it is you must release in order for this to be done."

The sacrifice. When the Varelos didn't reply to that, she knew she was right. *I have no idea what that is. And if you're about to tell me it has to be Romeo, you can forget about it.*

"I do not forget." The myriad voices rose and faded together, leaving her in the silence and the increasing rate of her heartbeat. *"Each magical calling themselves a part of The Black Heron Society already gave what they cherished in order to become what they are. My power cannot open that door for you. I am not of you. This sacrifice must have*

meaning. It must cause you some measure of grief to relinquish."

Whatever I have to give up, there's no way it would be anywhere near as important to me as my mom is.

"Or perhaps it is."

The tingling buzz shooting up her arms intensified and pulsed like her heartbeat. The same images the golden tree had given her filled the bright-white canvas of nothing all around her. The second they faded again, she knew. *That's all? I have to sacrifice the tree?*

"That is part of it. You are connected to more than you may realize in this life, Optatus. The tree is a final gift from your mother. It is the source of love and of the suffering you have endured since it was called into being. The tree brought you here to it, which perhaps you might not have achieved had you not possessed a certain omniscient artifact."

Omniscient, huh? You're talking about yourself, aren't you? Her lips twitched into the ghost of a smile.

"Indeed. You cannot remain the one who wields the Varelos if you are to do what you came to this place to do."

For a few seconds, her mind raced faster than she could put into words, despite the fact that the magical weapon could actually read her mind when she communed with it like this. *I can't simply give you to someone else. The Black Heron would try to take you from me anyway, and there's no way I can let that happen.* When the artifact made no reply again, she added, *Who gets to wield the Varelos after me, then?*

"That is for the Optatus who wields it now to decide."

Great. I'm gonna have to take a minute to think about that one.

"*Time is running short.*"

Yeah, I know. Her fingers tightened around the copper rod. *Okay. First things first, then. I still need to cast that spell for Romeo. To protect him. You know the one I'm talking about.*

"*Yes.*"

Then comes the sacrifice. I assume I have to cut this tree down. At this point, no answer from the Varelos' chorus of voices might as well have been a definitive yes too. *And then I have to give you away. I don't have time to find someone else to take you.*

"*I have been hidden before.*"

Yeah, but not on the doorstep of a society full of crazies who want to turn the whole magical world upside down.

"*Again, Optatus, the decision is yours.*"

I know. You've told me that from the very beginning. I'll think of something.

With a little more effort this time, knowing she wouldn't have the Varelos with her for much longer to call on whenever she wanted, she severed the connection. The desert heat and the sharp grittiness of so much sand under her clothes and sticking to her skin returned at once. It didn't surprise her when a little more of her sleep-deprived exhaustion returned with it.

She dropped the artifact into her lap and sighed.

"Is everything okay?" Romeo's voice came from beside her, his shadow still over her as she sat there with her eyes closed.

With a deep breath, Lily rubbed her eyes and blinked the sand out of them. "Yep. I think that oasis water is starting to wear off."

"Hey, when we finish this and get your mom out of there, you can sleep for however long you want."

She laughed and opened her eyes fully as he ran a gentle hand over her shoulder. "That sounds like a good plan. I only have a few more things to do first."

"Like actually get her out. Yeah, I know." It took him a few seconds, but he finally realized she was looking at him with a little more amusement than the thought of rescuing Greta Antony probably warranted. "What?"

"I meant a few things I have to do right now. With you."

"Okay..." He glanced at the Winnie and smirked. "Maybe we should save the private celebration for after—"

She snorted and raised the Varelos. "The spell, Romeo. To keep you safe once we're inside."

"Right." He eyed the bend of the U shape at the tip of the copper rod as she slowly aimed it at his chest. "I can't lie. That's not as exciting as what I was thinking. Do you want me to stand up or something?"

"No...you should probably stay right there. I don't wanna knock you over or anything." His wide eyes made her chuckle. "I'm kidding. Mostly. I've never done this spell before, but I know the Varelos knows what it's doing."

"Right. It knows."

"That's not simply a figure of speech. Ready?"

Romeo shrugged and looked at the artifact. "Sure.

Why not? Massively powerful weapon pointed right at my chest. Let's do it."

"Okay." Closing her eyes again, she drew the power she needed from the Varelos and turned the spell over and over in her mind. *The power of my mirror-necklace. From within and without, and I'm the one who has to put it there.* When she felt the pressure of the artifact pressed lightly against his chest, she raised her other hand to brush her fingers against the silver-framed mirror at her throat. The charm made her fingers tingle before a cool streak of energy jolted down her arm and through her body, into the Varelos, and into his chest.

When he sucked in a sharp breath, she opened her eyes. The copper rod pulsed with a faint silver light where it touched him. He stared at that light as it spread from the center of his chest and encompassed his entire body before it faded.

The tingle left her hand completely, and the artifact felt like another metal tool in her grasp.

"There." She nodded.

Romeo slowly raised his head to meet her gaze. "That felt like a cold shower."

"Well, hopefully, it got your mind off of how we'll celebrate this when we're done." She smirked and searched his gaze. "How do you feel?"

"Totally normal. Regular Romeo." He grinned. "That's it?"

"Yep." *I gave him his own personal mirror charm to undo the most powerful mistake. I hope I'm right about what that's gonna be.*

"Cool." He leaned away from the tip of the Varelos and pushed himself to his feet. "I honestly expected much worse. Maybe it's not so bad after all."

Lily accepted his hand to help her off the ground and ducked to avoid snagging her hair on the glowing branches of the tree. "It's not so bad. But you're not getting your hands on it."

He raised his hands in surrender. "Hey, I didn't say I want it. Even if you gave it to me."

"It's a good thing I wasn't considering it, then." Stepping away from the tree, she held the Varelos even tighter and stopped. "Maybe that's not what it meant. I don't think I have to give it to anyone."

"Uh...if you start calling that thing My Precious, we're gonna have a real problem."

She cut him a glance full of mock insult. "Come on. I know I haven't slept for four days but comparing me to Gollum is taking it a little too far."

Romeo faked surprise. "I would never—wait. What do you mean that's not what it meant?"

"Right. Time for a recap." She nodded at the artifact and gazed up at the tree. "Basically, because I'm not already a Black Heron member—hurray for me—I have to make a sacrifice to pull up that orange-brown wall and get through it. Whatever it is."

He immediately scowled. "It had to be a sacrifice."

"Not the kind you're thinking. Something that has meaning and that's important to me. Don't worry, I already crossed you off the list." She sent him a winning grin and almost laughed when he tried to hide his sigh of relief. "It has two parts. The first is this tree."

"That's a bummer."

Lily shrugged. "I have everything I needed from it anyway, so that's fine. Although it looks really cool standing here in the middle of the Sahara. The second part is that I can't keep this."

They both stared at the Varelos as she lifted it in her hand. Romeo wrinkled his nose. "You can't simply give it away, either."

"I know. That's not what's gonna happen anyway." She tipped the copper rod from one side to the other in her hand and it glinted in the sunlight. "But be ready for whatever happens after I finish both parts, okay?"

"Right. This'll be like one giant knock on the front door—in a place we're definitely not supposed to be."

She grinned at him and nodded. "Yep. And I should probably get this done before all the energy from that special oasis water drains out of me completely."

"I'm ready when you are, Lil."

"Good." When she tightened her grasp on the Varelos, the copper rod sent a flare of cool, energetic magic into her fingertips. It was connected to her now, in whatever way it could be, and read her intentions with perfect clarity without her having to tap into that meditative conversation space.

With a deep breath, she stretched forward to set it gently against the glowing bark of the tree her mom had left for her in the desert. The golden light flared even brighter for a second before it winked out completely.

Without it, the tree looked naked and dead. The tips of the highest branches darkened into an ash-gray and then black. The rest of the tree followed suit, and everywhere the blackness appeared, the bark and the structure of the tree itself crumbled into tiny specs of black dust. A wind kicked up again in the desert, and in under ten seconds, they stood in a storm of swirling golden sand and the blackened flakes of the destroyed tree—all that remained of Greta Antony's last gift.

"Woah." Romeo stared at the pile of black dust in front of them.

"Yeah, that actually wasn't as bad as I expected. It's merely closing one door to open another, right?" She nodded and stepped toward where she thought the orange-brown wall of the Black Heron's wards waited for her. "Now for the big one."

She closed her eyes and connected with the Varelos as the rod sent prickling waves up her arm. The desert around her vanished to be replaced by the blinding whiteness. *I guess this is the last time I'll be doing this. Ever.*

"*You have made your decision, then?*" The voices almost sounded tired.

Yeah, but you still need to make yours.

"*I decide whatever my wielder requests of me.*"

Lily took a deep breath. *Still, I have to ask. How do you feel about pressing the self-destruct button?*

"*I have existed for thousands of years and been wielded by warriors and peacemakers, leaders, paupers, and heroes. I have withstood the test of time in this world and seen the successes and the devastation brought about by all its people. You speak of using my power to destroy its very source."*

Yep. If I can't keep you—and I really don't have the time to go looking for another god's temple to hide you in—I can't simply leave you out here. I can't take you with me, either. Bringing you to the Black Heron would be a really stupid mistake. But I won't turn back now. So, maybe the last sacrifice is yours. How about it?

There was a long pause, and she almost took it as consent although she didn't know how to proceed with pressing the proverbial self-destruct button. When the hundreds of voices returned, there was definite amusement in their tones.

"I believe that is the best command anyone has given me in a very long time, Optatus. Thank you for the opportunity to have served you."

Well, thanks for keeping me sane over the last few days. I guess we helped each other out that way. Ready?

"Quite."

She took a deep breath. Okay, then. On the count of three, I guess. One...two...

TEN

The tingling buzz that seared up Lily's arm encompassed her entire body now and made her think for a second that she'd actually been electrocuted. The Varelos ejected her from their communication and brought the desert around her once more with intense heat and unbearable brightness. She cried out when the artifact launched itself out of her hand and rocketed away to stop a few yards from her where it hovered there in midair.

"Lily?" Romeo stared at the magical weapon, his voice low. "What's going on?"

"I don't—"

A massive crack rent the air and echoed as loudly as if they stood in a cave instead of in the open surrounded by nothing but sand. A brilliant white light exploded from the center of the Varelos to form an orb the size of the Winnie around the artifact. This burst apart and shot in every direction like a massive shock wave.

The ground rocked beneath them, and she stumbled

sideways before the wave of blinding white magic struck her in the chest. It catapulted across the sand and hurled Romeo off his feet too. The Winnie groaned and rocked against the blast, pelted by sand and dust and wind stirred up by the Varelos' final act. A thunderous roar filled the air, and she rolled over onto her side to cover her ears with both hands. She thought her teeth would fall out of her head with the vibrating power of that sound. Maybe she screamed, too, although she couldn't be sure. Sand kicked up everywhere and swirled around the place where the Varelos had hovered.

The werewolf scrambled toward her on his hands and knees, gritting his teeth against the force of the magical weapon's energy released all around them. He could barely see through the manufactured dust storm, but he reached her and huddled over her, ready to protect her with his own body if he had to. "What's happening?" he shouted, but he couldn't even hear himself.

Her eyes were clenched shut and her mouth open in a silent scream. Or maybe it was only silent beneath the pounding roar and the howling wind that tried to bury them in the sand.

In the next moment, everything stopped.

The wind died, the sand sifted earthward to find a new place on the desert floor, and two hollow thumps sounded from directly in front of them. Breathing heavily, the young couple looked up from where they'd huddled to see the copper rod lying in the sand a few yards away—broken cleanly in half.

Romeo gaped in disbelief. "Did you actually break the

most powerful magical weapon in the history of magical weapons?"

Lily wiped the sand off her face and had to spit a few times to get most of it out of her mouth. "It's more like I told it to break itself."

"And it had to do what you said."

"Basically. I actually think it wanted to be destroyed—to simply not exist anymore."

"Yeah, maybe being immortal and all-powerful isn't what it's cracked up to be." He shook his head and studied her. "Are you okay?"

"I'm fine. But I'm not sure what's supposed to happen now."

Right on cue, the air on the other side of the broken Varelos shimmered and emitted a high-pitched whine. The wavering, orange-brown wall from her visions and the Black Heron network revealed itself only a few yards away without a sound.

"It worked." Her eyes lit up as she stared at the wards in front of her, now present in her reality and not only in images she'd been seeing for weeks. "We did it."

With a wry chuckle, Romeo pushed himself to his feet and helped her to stand beside him. "I stood here and watched on this one, Lil. You did all the work."

"It honestly wasn't that hard." She bit her lip and stared at the shimmering wall. "This feels too easy."

"We'll find out once we're on the other side."

"I guess." She pulled her gaze away from the warded wall when he took her hand. "Ready?"

"Oh, yeah. Let's get this done."

They stepped forward together and a ball of purple magic churned past them from behind and buried itself in the sand. Huge sheets of it sprayed up against the young witch and her werewolf companion.

"You're not going anywhere."

They whirled to see three magicals standing between them and the Winnebago. The woman who'd thrown the warning spell summoned another ball of purple energy and tossed it in her hand. "That was quite the message you sent."

Romeo uttered a deep growl, his eyes flashing silver.

"I didn't send a message," she said. Her favorite sparking red attack spell flared at her fingertips.

"Oh yes, you did." A hulking man with shaggy brown hair and a yellow-white beard flexed his fingers. "You can't hide a bomb in the desert, especially when it triggers those protection wards behind you. We've all been waiting for those to go off." The man sneered to reveal yellowed teeth. When he grunted and stretched his fingers fully, his fingernails jutted into glinting, two-inch claws, although the rest of him didn't change.

"Great." Lily glanced at her companion as he glared at their unwelcome visitors, his lips twisted in a warning snarl. "More Black Heron mutants."

"Seeing as we got here first," the woman added, "we get to have a little fun with you before everyone else. First come, first served, and all that."

"Nice try."

The minute she saw the witch launch the next attack, she dove to the side and released her own attack spell.

Romeo snarled and shifted, leaving his clothes behind in a sandy pile. The mutant werewolf roared and charged across the sand, his muscles rippling and bulging beneath his shirt, but he never fully took another shape.

The third Black Heron member who'd appeared with the other magicals shouted something unintelligible and raised a hand toward Lily. When nothing happened, she turned her attention to the other witch who continued to fire purple shots at her. With both hands, the Optatus launched another attack, but her adversary blocked them with a hastily constructed shield. It wasn't a very effective one, though, and the witch shouted in pain and shook her hand where the spell had managed to penetrate.

"It looks like you're not quite ready for that one." Lily dispatched another round of red attack spells. Shouting in anger now, the Black Heron witch ducked the first few shots and skidded awkwardly in the sand. The next one would have caught her, but she saw the mutant magical struggling with his spells from the corner of her eye. A bright-green dart finally burst from his open hand and rocketed toward her. She raised a warded shield to deflect it and missed hitting the witch with her last volley of attacks.

Somewhere beside her, Romeo darted and scrambled in the sand as he snapped his jaws at the werewolf hybrid who still walked upright on two legs. His adversary was too slow to defend against all of the black wolf's attacks, but he packed a strong enough punch when his fist connected with one of Romeo's hips.

The air crackled with electric pops as two more Black

Heron members teleported in. Five more followed, then another three, and finally, a whole den of warlocks who apparently tried to change the warlock look by all having spiked their hair into ridiculously huge mohawks. Each one of them raised a hand to release a blood-red mist that spilled across the desert.

Lily ducked beneath another green dart from the mutant magical with spellcasting issues and raised a warded shield to deflect a ball of purple attack spell and a handful of muddy brown slop that was probably supposed to be some kind of nefarious magical gas. "What is going on?"

Two witches sprinted clumsily across the sand toward the battle between the black wolf and the mutant. Romeo had his jaws clamped around the hybrid's bulging forearm and yanked with powerful shakes of his head. Lily launched two quick bursts of the sharp, knifelike spell she'd learned in a magical bar in Canada. Yellow streaks of light slashed across the witches' thighs as they hurtled toward the werewolf. Both men cried out and fell in the sand. One of them sent a cracking explosion of flames shooting toward the Black Heron's orange-brown wards but they snuffed out upon contact.

More oddly dressed, angry, snarling, mutated hybrid magicals popped into existence with each passing second. Each of them at first tried to reach Lily until they began to fling spells at each other simply to get their neighbors out of the way.

Romeo released the mutant and it stumbled forward in time to catch the full brunt of the electrical charges two witches with orange-streaked hair had aimed at the black wolf. It roared within the blue net of energy and keeled over, twitching in the sand. The werewolf growled and surged after the closest attacker, sending up sprays of sand behind him with each bound.

Lily had knocked over two of the closest society members with her compulsive force—and might have bashed their heads together in the process—when she noticed the warlocks' combined blood magic drifting quickly toward her across the sand. The red mist crackled and sparked but didn't slow. A witch with bulging yellow eyes and a scar along her neck stepped forward toward her and the minute her foot touched the mist, she shrieked and crumpled.

Stepping back toward the warded wall, she studied the mist warily and almost clapped her hands to release the black cloud of her Optatus magic. Despite the urge to do so, she didn't. *"Make them think the night has already come,"* the wandering spirit had told her. Wiping out the Black Heron's experimenting rebels would blow up her entire Plan A, and Plan B didn't exist.

Instead, she stepped away from the crawling mist and deflected the barrage of attack spells that actually found their way to her. She hurled a few darts of sparkling red attacks and the slashing yellow knifelike spells toward the den of warlocks and followed it up with two of her strongest compulsion blasts. Apparently, the warlocks had put up their own permanent shield. Red sparks and yellow streaks of light bounced off the shimmering air in front of the mohawked magicals, but her force attacks did the trick.

She didn't get to see the three warlocks in front stagger back against those gathered behind them. A whip of green, writhing magic coiled around her wrist and seared the already raw marks left there by the shackles her mom had worn for weeks. Lily cried out in pain and was jerked sideways by the wielder of the magical whip. Someone cackled not too far away, but the sound cut off abruptly when a huge, shaggy black wolf pounced on the society member and dug his claws into her throat.

Gritting her teeth, Lily aimed the yellow light of razor-sharp magic at the whip and severed it cleanly. The coiled strand withered and fell from around her wrist but now, an angry red burn wound up her skin. Another group of Black Heron members teleported into the desert, screaming and whooping some kind of battle cry as they threw spells in every direction. There were too many to count now, and it wasn't like the young couple could simply board the Winnie and drive away from the chaos. They had already come this far to reach their destination. *The black cloud might be the only choice I have.*

Behind her, the orange-brown wall of warded magic flashed a pale orange light. The high-pitched whine she'd heard when the Varelos had revealed the Black Heron's final gateway returned, but it now rose to a deafening volume. Some of the rebel members stopped at the sound and forgot their quarrels and Lily as they turned and stared at the wall. The remainder simply continued to pummel each other with magic.

A chorus of growls rose from the wall behind her. Lily spun again to see a pack of entirely white wolves darting across the sand. The last few of them leaped through the warded wall, their teeth bared and red eyes glowing brightly even under the desert sun.

"What is happening?" Lily whispered.

Behind them came a dozen more magicals who raced into the fray. She stepped sideways along the wall and away from them. The Black Heron members who'd come from the place she was trying to go unleashed a furious volley of attacks—on their fellow members.

The air crackled with an excess of magic in one place and the sand dunes around them flared in flashing colors while the flattened sand where they fought soaked up pools of blood. The white wolves were nothing more than streaks between bodies that destroyed mutant and hybrid magicals on every side. The other society members who'd come to fight their faction of peons gone rogue didn't make a sound as they unleashed their wrath. Amidst shrieking cries of agony, snarls, snapping bones, and the whir, hiss, crack, and roar of so many spells striking so many targets, Lily found herself completely forgotten by everyone.

Except for Romeo. The black wolf had noticed the turn of this surprise battle and now padded quickly across the sand toward her. He stopped at her side, panting, and his silver eyes reflected the burst of colored spells that exploded in every direction. Lily stepped toward him and dug her fingers into the thick, coarse fur of his neck to make sure he was real and she wasn't imagining the rest of it.

More movement by the wall caught her eye. The last person to step through it was a tall man with dark hair and a dark goatee. He wore a velvet smoking jacket, even in the Saharan heat, the wide collar turned down over his shoulders. He raised his hand and cast an entire shower of green flames across the desert turned battlefield. None of them landed on any of the society members who'd joined him from the other side of the wall.

More screams followed, and the last few rebels who could still breathe and move soon lost even that ability. The only sound was the hiss of damp sand under burned bodies, the crackle of green flames still lapping at clothes, and a few dying gasps. The victors took their time to walk amongst the fallen to ensure they're done a thorough job of it.

The man in the smoking jacket turned his head with a wry smile to look at the young couple. His fake eye sparkled in the sunlight. "That was quite an entrance you made for yourself."

Lily's mouth dropped open. *Did he bring a small army to help us?*

One of the bodies still burning beneath the green flames pushed itself to its feet and barreled toward the man with one eye. A muffled, agonized wail escaped the magical's throat, his whole body ablaze and even his face obscured by the fire. Lily glanced at the wayward society member on a suicide mission, whom the one-eyed man seemed not to notice. A white blur streaked through the air and pounced upon the screaming magical. A quick struggle was accompanied by a few muffled grunts, followed a sharp, jarring crunch and silence.

The one-eyed man's smile widened, and he shook his

head as if that would erase the minor interruption. "I've put up with their special brand of idiocy for much longer than I should have. But now that you're here, none of it matters."

Romeo's hackles rose beneath her hand, even before he uttered a low, warning growl. She raised her hand from his fur and summoned another attack spell, holding it low against her hip. "I'm here for Greta Antony."

The one-eyed man inclined his head. "Of course you are. I've known that for quite some time. As I expect you've known that we've been waiting for you, Lily. Please." He extended a hand toward the orange-brown wall of the Black Heron Society's wards and turned halfway toward them. "Come with me."

No attacks and a polite invitation. Definitely not what I expected. She glanced at Romeo, who'd stopped growling now to look at her and meet her gaze. Her focus shifted to the one-eyed man and she stepped away from the wall toward the bodies scattered all over this unknown part of the Sahara. The other society members watched her intently as she picked her way through the bodies toward the place she thought Romeo had shifted. There they were —his clothes crumpled in a heap and half-buried in the sand. She stooped to pick up his shirt and jeans and turned away from the puff of sand and who knew what else when she shook them out. He'd have to go barefoot from here on out.

No one moved when she made her way back toward the one-eyed man. Romeo hadn't even turned to watch her but still stared at the magical who thought he'd play at a warm, inviting host. She stopped beside the black wolf and held the clothes out toward him as she sent a sidelong look at the waiting man. "I'd get used to having sand in your clothes. Sorry."

The society leader chuckled and clasped his hands behind his back. "Shall we?"

"Where's Greta?"

"Your mother's safe, Lily. I can assure you of that now. Come with me and I'll show you." He nodded toward the warded wall and glanced at the bright, searing sky. "I'm overdressed for this place." His lips squeaked when he sucked on his teeth. "We'll wait for you on the other side but don't take too long." With that, he turned and stepped through the warded wall, leaving behind a shimmering ripple like he'd stepped into a lake.

The other Black Heron members moved at the same time and walked across the sand and the bodies to follow the one-eyed man. A few of them glanced at Lily with raised eyebrows, either in curiosity or warning. The others simply stared straight ahead and marched like soldiers through the wall. The white wolves moved quickly and silently and none of them spared so much as a glance or a sniff at the black-furred outsider in their midst.

When the last of them had disappeared, Romeo shifted and pulled his clothes out of Lily's hand as he stood. "Out of all the weird things, Lil, that takes the cake."

"Yeah…" She stared at the wall and waited until he'd zipped his jeans before she turned to look at him. "This feels like a trap."

"Definitely."

"We have to keep going."

"I know. I'm all in." He tried to brush the remaining sand off his t-shirt but quickly gave up. "Is your arm okay?"

She glanced at the fresh burn around her wrist. "Yeah, it's fine. Romeo." He looked at her again with wide eyes, and she took a deep breath. "Don't forget, okay? Whatever happens, whatever I do or say or what you think you see, don't forget what I told you."

He raised his hand to her sand-dusted cheek and nodded. "I'll tell 'em all to go to hell. Got it."

"Okay. Let's go."

Together, they turned toward the shimmering wall in the desert and stepped through to where the Black Heron Society waited for them.

ELEVEN

When they emerged on the other side of the wall, Lily first thought that they were in some kind of cave. Everything was black stone, rising high all around them. The circular walls of this apparent fortress rose impossibly high—much higher than the tallest point of the building in the center that was half stronghold and half temple. That too was made of black stone, as were the smaller outbuildings in a ring around the center. Even the ground beneath their feet wasn't really ground but more of the same hard, cold, glistening black rock.

But there was still light. She craned her neck to see what had to be a blue sky above, although it was paler than it should have been. "The wards go way higher than the walls," she whispered.

Romeo followed her gaze and frowned. "That doesn't look right."

"It's not. I don't think we're even in the desert anymore."

"Well, it's not Kansas, either." When Lily stared at him, he shrugged. "This is not the time for jokes. I get it."

"Welcome to the High Seat." The one-eyed man stepped toward them from the group of waiting magicals a few yards away. "I think I can speak for everyone here when I say I'm glad you finally found your way to us, Lily."

"You don't speak for everyone here."

At her words, his eyes widened. "Of course not. Greta Antony's daughter wouldn't let anyone speak for her, would she? What about him?" He nodded toward Romeo.

The werewolf simply gave her a blank look, so she said, "He's with me."

"Hmm." The one-eyed man squinted at her, his glass eye glinting even in the low light of this place. "That's not really what I meant, but we'll get to that part when it's time. I bet you're really ready to get started. And so am I." He rubbed his hands together, then gave the fakest little start like he'd forgotten all about the normal niceties of sane people meeting each other for the first time. "Oh, I'm sorry. My name's Carmichael."

Lily stared at his hand extended toward her but didn't take it. "You said you'd take me to my mom."

His lips twitched, then he grinned. "Yes, I did. Let's go." He nodded toward the center of the walled-in fortress that looked more like a giant chamber.

The young couple shared a glance and the werewolf leaned toward her. "You're trying to piss him off, aren't you?"

She stared at the band of society members following Carmichael as she and Romeo slowly stepped into line behind them. "It's not that hard," she muttered. "He doesn't expect us to buy this fake welcome. And I wouldn't expect him to believe me if I acted like I didn't see right through it."

"He thinks he can flatter you into joining them." He stuck his hands in his pockets and kept his gaze on the cold black stone beneath his bare feet.

"Or at least agree to their spell, yeah. It's a little late for that, though."

"So what's the plan, then, Lil? He takes us to your mom, and what? We simply blast our way out of a secret fortress in the middle of who knows where and somehow make it past all the magicals stashed away in this place? Those white wolves aren't full werewolf. And I'm not sure I can outrun them. Not for very long, at least."

Lily shook her head. "Werewolf and warlock. I didn't know what they were first, but the white and the red eyes... That has to be what they are."

"They haven't shifted, though."

"I know."

They both studied the white wolves that padded silently on either side of them as the small procession moved across the black stone toward the stronghold in the center of the Black Heron's walled city. If she hadn't actually been a part of it, Lily wouldn't have known that all these magicals walking in front of her had fought a battle that was more like a slaughter. *It feels like we're all simply out for a stroll.*

They didn't see anyone else as they moved through the High Seat. Even when they passed between two of the smaller outbuildings—which had no doors and held no light at all inside—the place felt empty. Nothing about it felt right, but she hadn't expected anything else. When they finally reached the front doors of the central castle-like building, Carmichael gave a quick flick of his wrist and kept walking. The huge double doors of black iron opened inward at his command, and he led them all inside.

The minute Lily and Romeo brought up the rear and stepped inside, the doors closed behind them with a loud bang. The society members who'd left the High Seat to rescue the newcomers—only to bring them inside and most likely torture them—moved away in every direction and went about their business as if the last twenty minutes had never happened.

Carmichael turned on his heels to face his wary guests and spread his arms. "So. What do you think?"

Lily studied the high, vaulted ceilings, the marble pillars and floors, and the tall vases of exotic plants along every wall. An indoor fountain splashed somewhere on her left, and the giant, opulent entryway was dotted with small groupings of leather couches and armchairs, pillows, and rugs. There was a standing fireplace on either side of the entryway in the large rooms, although the hearths were empty.

"It's warmer." That was the only thing she could think of to say.

"Yes. Well, those of us who are committed to our goals at the High Seat spend most of our time in this very building. It might be a small city all on its own, come to think of it. It'll grow on you."

A round of laughter broke out in the open lounge room on their right, where a group of society members sat in high-backed chairs around a pristinely glossy wooden table, sipping out of highball glasses and enjoying themselves. None of them looked at the new guests in the entryway.

"I think your intuition's a little off, there." Lily turned her attention back to Carmichael. "The only reason I'm here is because you took my mom and you've held her prisoner in your small city."

"Let's make this perfectly clear, Lily." He straightened his shoulders and took a step toward her. "I did not take Greta. I haven't set foot outside these walls in a very long time until today. And I have not tortured anyone. Your mother is perfectly safe and perfectly happy, considering everything she's been through. I'm happy to facilitate your reunion with her, but it would be nice to receive a few simple courtesies in return. Especially before you've even had a chance to see what I've been preparing for you. Can you do that?" The man's nostrils flared when he raised an eyebrow, his smile twisted on a mouth that had not learned what a real smile should be.

"I can." Lily held his gaze. *What's he playing at?* "But only if you take me to her right now. I definitely don't need a tour."

"Fair enough." The one-eyed man inclined his head and clasped his hands behind his back as he waited for her to keep up her end of this ridiculous deal.

She glanced around and finally nodded at the tree in a gray marble planter. "Nice ficus."

Carmichael looked at the plant and chuckled. "That's a start. Thank you." He turned and headed swiftly down the long hall of the entryway. "Keep up, then."

She tried to ignore Romeo's inquisitive stare, but he made it impossible when he bumped the back of his hand against hers.

"Are we pretending to be polite guests, now?"

"I guess." She eyed the random pockets of society members gathered throughout the open rooms on either side, none of whom looked at them as they moved quickly and silently after Carmichael. "But be ready. I have no idea what these people are up to, but it can't be this easy."

"I coulda told you that." He stared at a werewolf with glowing purple eyes and a fairy—the first they'd seen who hadn't been with the Black Heron either in the skirmish outside the fortress or within its interior—standing in front of a dartboard mounted on the standing fireplace. The fairy's hair shimmered from bright green to blood-red and back again as he threw five darts into the bullseye. The werewolf's groan of irritation followed them as they left the entryway.

"There's an arboretum down this hall." Carmichael pointed to the left without turning. "It has a little garden, both for food and for ingredients. They feed into the potions labs a little farther down."

Lily rolled her eyes. *We're actually getting a tour.*

The main room and marble floors stopped at a gigantic staircase, also of marble, that stretched up to a mid-point landing before branching to the left and the right. The intricately worked wrought-iron banisters glinted in the bright light from the chandelier overhead. Lily thought she saw tiny creatures forged into the winding spirals of the banister post.

"The private quarters are upstairs," Carmichael said. "That's most of the second floor on this wing. It's not where we're headed, though." He waved them to the right, where another hallway branched out from the main room.

"The place has wings," Romeo muttered and raised his eyebrows.

Lily merely scowled and didn't want to think about exactly how big this place really was.

"The library is at the end of this corridor." Carmichael waved ahead of them. "Not everything has been added to our shelves the way I would have hoped, but for the most part, we have what we need. The meditation room is beside it. Thaddeus originally wanted that to be the sparring rooms, but the man couldn't see a stupid idea if it bit him in the ass. Which it normally did." He chuckled. "The sparring rooms are on the other side of the potions labs." He looked over his shoulder to give his guests a coy smile.

Romeo nudged Lily with his elbow and reminded her of their deal.

"Naturally." She said the words, but they lacked any hint of enthusiasm.

Carmichael tilted his head and turned left into another branching corridor. This one was much wider and dimly lit by round globes every few feet along the glistening walls. When he stopped at a set of nine-foot-tall double doors of deep cherrywood, his smile had disappeared beneath lips pressed firmly together. "I'd very much enjoy giving you the rest of the tour later, of course. Or you may choose to explore certain areas yourself, in your own time. For now, as promised, you've finally come to the place you've been seeking for months now, Lily."

The corners of the man's mouth twitched upward into an obviously false smile, then fell into their usual expression.

I don't think he likes this any more than I do. Too much pressure to get what he wants. Lily couldn't think of anything polite to say, so instead of breaking their tenuous deal, she merely nodded at the double doors.

TWELVE

Without taking his dark eye off her, Carmichael snapped his fingers. The doors opened slowly with a low, echoing groan that whispered across the wooden floors of the room beyond. The room was massive for what was essentially a glorified study. Bookshelves lined the walls on either side, each with two ladders hitched to tracks that led to metal catwalks to reach the books almost at the ceiling. A massive fireplace took up the center of the left-hand wall. The back wall beneath the vaulted ceiling was a huge pane of stained glass, although the only colors in it were white and black—a white background behind a black heron with a twelve-foot wingspan that stretched all the away across.

Where is she? Lily scanned the room. Study tables stood beside the bookshelves. Desk lamps boasted shades of emerald-green glass. Wing-backed armchairs were placed in the center of the room, their backs to her with a bearskin rug beneath them. A very large couch opposite the chairs could have seated eight people at once. For a second, she thought this was a trick.

"You said—"

She stopped when something stirred within the couch's dozens of pillows in deep red, black, and gold. A black shawl slipped from Greta Antony's shoulders as she stood from the couch and revealed the emerald-green dress beneath it.

Without a word, Lily half-ran around the armchairs toward her mom's open arms. She wanted to throw herself into them and never let go of the woman she'd finally found. But she slowed a few feet away when she got a better look.

Greta's eyes were dull beneath heavy, half-closed lids. The dark circles under them were gone. Her smile looked weak and exhausted despite the fact that her blonde hair had been washed, brushed, and settled almost theatrically over her shoulders. And she simply stood there, her arms raised a little in welcome, but she didn't step forward to embrace her daughter.

"Mom?"

"Don't make me wait all day for a hug, sweets." Greta inclined her head and nodded slowly.

Hearing that nickname from her mom's lips was the only proof she needed that this actually was Greta Antony and not a Black Heron member standing there behind an elaborate illusion charm. Her heart and head fought against her body as she stepped jerkily toward Greta and wrapped her arms around her mom's thin frame. The green dress—more of a gown that fell all the way to the floor with long sleeves hanging slightly past her hands—was incredibly soft and cool. She squeezed her but stopped quickly when she felt the lack of strength in her mother's arms around her.

"I found you," she whispered and pressed her cheek against her clean hair. It had a floral smell to it—sweet at first and not unpleasant, but beneath the sweetness was the unmistakable scent of smoke.

Greta patted her daughter's back gently, then took her by the shoulders and pushed them a little apart. Everything about her looked wrong when she gazed into her eyes. "You found me. We knew you would. Carmichael's been watching you for some time." One of her eyelids twitched, and Lily stiffened.

She's telling me he's still watching and still listening. Despite the disheartening surprise of seeing her mom like this, she knew there was more to it than the way the Black Heron had dressed Greta Antony to play whatever part she was there to play. There had to be. "Are you okay?"

"Oh..." The woman's light laughter didn't even remotely pass for genuine. "Of course. Look at me. Look at you." She passed a hand over her daughter's head, ran it down her mussed hair coated with sand, and patted her shoulder.

"You look...not like I expected." She couldn't say her mom looked different than when they'd spoken to each other in the handful of visions over the last few weeks. *Carmichael might not know about those yet.* She stepped away and glanced at the emerald-green dress again. It looked like it belonged in the thirteenth-century High-lands, not there.

"Well, I hope it's a nice surprise." Greta nodded slowly. "They've treated me very well here."

Lily glanced sharply up at her and swallowed. That didn't sound anything like Greta at all. *A nice surprise?* Maybe the Black Heron had treated her mom well compared to the way they'd treated her for over six months now. But Lily had the manacle burns on her wrists—received only a few days before the angry welt from a magical slap—to prove that it wasn't all dresses and combed hair and lazy smiles.

Trying to hide her concern, she swallowed. "It's definitely a surprise."

"Ah." Carmichael stepped toward them, and Lily wanted to turn around and blast him across the room. She managed to restrain herself because that would ruin everything. "I understand this may come as something of a shock to you, Lily. But once Greta came to fully understand what we're trying to do here—what we need you to help us accomplish—she was more than willing to agree to our terms. As a result, she has a seat of honor at the ritual when that day comes. And it will very soon. Your mother has access here to anything she could possibly want or need. Attendants to wait on her. There are feasts at any time of day. The respect of the Black Heron at the High Seat and everyone who knows what she's done to bring us that much closer to our goals."

She stared at him and couldn't get her face to do anything that might hide her bafflement. *Does he think I'm so stupid?* Her mom would never wear a dress like that or talk about how well she'd been treated after months of torture—months she'd spent looking for her daughter with her raven totem and fighting every chance she had to escape.

The young witch and the apparent leader of the Black Heron Society stared impassively at each other.

Greta stepped slowly toward them and gestured at the double doors again. "Would you like to see the genius behind what he's doing?"

Lily glanced behind Carmichael at the entrance to this embellished study. Romeo stood inside the doors where she'd left him, his eyes wide and his mouth open in complete disbelief. *At least I'm not the only one who's not buying this.*

"I didn't come to see what he's doing." She fought to keep her words at normal speaking volumes. "I came here to find you, Mom, and take you home."

"Well, I..." Greta lowered her gaze and shook her head almost imperceptibly. "I really think—"

"You've come all this way." Carmichael set a hand on Lily's shoulder and she immediately shrugged it off and stepped back. Either he'd gotten the exact reaction he'd wanted out of her, or he decided to ignore her breaking their little deal about politeness. "You should stay, Lily. At least for a few days. Take a look at what we have to offer here and what we're preparing to set into motion. Your mom has finally come around to seeing things as we do. You will too."

"I'm fairly sure everyone in this room already knows

that's not gonna happen." She scowled at the man. "Did you drug her?"

He chuckled, but it was slick and oily and insincere. "That's completely unnecessary. Greta came to these conclusions all on her own. Eventually."

Lily stared at her mom, who stood in the weird green dress, her blonde hair curtaining both sides of her face as she gazed blankly at the floor with her hands clasped in front of her. *She's been like this for days. That's why I stopped feeling everything they did to her. But there's no way he broke her. No way.*

"How about this, Lily?" Carmichael spread his arms in a gesture of compromise. "Come with me. Your mother will join us for the whole thing if that makes you feel better. And if you still haven't changed your mind by the time I've finished my little spiel, we'll do things your way."

The man's lips twitched again.

She looked at Romeo again. He rubbed the back of his neck in the telltale way he did when uncomfortable and stared at the trio beside the couch. When she caught his eye, he offered enough of a shrug that she knew he would have told her to take the opportunity. Not to learn more about what the Black Heron wanted—they already knew that—but to give them a chance to escape from there with her mom and as little violence as possible.

"Fine." Lily couldn't look at her deceiving host. "Show me whatever you have to show me. But I won't go anywhere without my mom."

"I wouldn't dream of separating you two now after how much time you've spent searching for her."

Carmichael grinned and the glass orb set in his eye socket flashed as the other eye gazed intently at her. "Follow me, then."

Greta stepped silently across the rug and slipped her hand into Lily's as he headed to the study's double doors. It was a brief moment of contact, barely enough to make her freeze. Her mom squeezed her hand before she pulled away and glided across the floor after her captor. She tried to read her face, looking for any clues, but the woman simply kept walking.

This isn't real. That's what she's telling me. This is only a game of lies and pretending for all three of us.

She nodded at Romeo. Her werewolf friend stepped toward her, but Carmichael raised a hand in front of his face and tsked. "No, no. You were not invited."

"I didn't know I needed an invitation." He growled warningly.

"For this, wolf, you do." Carmichael snapped his fingers, and two other society members stepped into the study. One of them was a huge bald man with no expression whatsoever. The other was half as tall, scrawny, and looked like a rat with blue hair. "Show our guest to the pack, if you would. And afford him every courtesy of an esteemed guest."

The society members stared at Romeo without a word, and Carmichael brushed past them out into the hall. Greta followed and paused briefly to study him. A small, sad smile lifted the corners of her mouth. "It's been a long time." With that, she followed Carmichael without waiting for a reply.

"Hey!" Lily sent Romeo a warning glance before she hurried out into the hall. "Hey, Romeo's coming with me."

"No, he's not." Carmichael didn't even turn.

"Then the deal's off. We do this my way right now."

The man started to turn until Romeo's voice echoed out into the hall. "Lily—"

"No." She tried to get to him on the other side of the doors, but the giant man whose face never moved stuck an arm out in front of the werewolf. It was a warning gesture. Everyone knew the man would physically hold him back if he fought. Lily scowled at the man and summoned her sparking attack spell. "I won't let them take you away. I don't know this place and I don't know these people."

"Lily." Romeo shook his head slowly as if to reassure her. "Go with them and take a look around, okay? There's no harm in that."

"Only if you're not with me—"

"Stop." He took a step back and spread his arms like that was the end of it. "I'll be fine. You heard what the guy said. Every courtesy. I guess I get to hang out with other werewolves too. We came in here prepared, remember? It's okay."

But it wasn't supposed to happen like this. These people should have locked us up by now.

He nodded at her and tapped his chest. Yep, the spell she'd cast on him with the Varelos definitely counted as being prepared.

"Miss Antony," Carmichael called from down the corridor.

She grimaced and nodded at him. "Okay. I'll find you when this tour's over. Promise."

"I know you will." He glanced at the huge man with his arm still held out like a railroad crossing block and winked at her.

With a deep breath, she pulled herself together and pointed at the society member with the incredibly long nose and beady eyes. "You guys had better play nice." She turned and followed her mother, who walked beside the man who had quite probably given the orders to abduct her and bring her all the way out there.

"Don't worry," Carmichael said as he moved down the hall again. "They'll take care of him."

"I'm not coming with you so we can talk about Romeo. Show me what you need to show me."

"Sure." The man nodded briefly and increased the pace.

Lily searched her mom's profile for any other hint of this game—a sign that Greta was still only going through the motions, showing Carmichael what he wanted to see. Her mom didn't reveal anything in the way she walked and her hands didn't move in some hidden gesture. She didn't even look at her daughter but instead, stared at the back of the man's head as they walked through the High Seat's fortress.

She's waiting for something else to happen. Now, I need to learn what that is before we can get out of here.

THIRTEEN

"All right, guys. Where's the party?" Romeo glanced from the tall man to his rat-faced companion and grinned. "You heard the man. Show me to the other wolves."

The larger of the two actually looked at him and finally lowered his arm. The smaller rolled his eyes and stepped toward the hall again. "As long as you stay behind me, you get to walk on your own two feet. If you try to run off or slip into rooms you're not supposed to, you and Frank are gonna get to know each other real well. Got it?"

"We're getting' to know each other already, aren't we?" The werewolf shrugged, and the man narrowed his eyes warningly. "Yeah, man. I got it."

"Good." His guide—or was it captor?—stepped into the hall and turned right.

Romeo followed him and glanced left to where Lily had disappeared with the Black Heron's leader and Greta

Antony. A quick shove from behind made him stumble and he spun around to shoot Frank a clueless shrug. "Okay, okay. He didn't say I couldn't look anywhere else."

"Well I'm saying it now," the apparent leader of the two muttered. "Get moving."

Frank grunted in warning, and the werewolf nodded before he followed. He couldn't keep track of all the turns they made or all the rooms they passed, although almost every door was shut. The open ones only gave a view of completely empty rooms, but they occasionally walked past the sounds of laughter and muted conversation.

The farther they walked, the dimmer the lights on the walls became. Neither of his escorts said anything to the few society members who crossed their path. When they passed a series of open doors, the sounds of spells being cast, bodies hurtling onto mats, and jeering shouts spilled out. Romeo peered inside to see a large group of magicals playing in what must have the sparring rooms Carmichael had mentioned. He couldn't catch any more than that before his head went fuzzy and he sneezed.

The rat-faced individual jumped and spun with a scowl. "What are you doing?"

"Sorry." Romeo sniffled and shook his head. "I only—" His second sneeze was so violent, he stumbled sideways in the darkened hallway.

"You've gotta be kidding me." The man darted a glance at Frank but received no response.

"What?" He shrugged and wiped his nose. "Have you never seen a werewolf around a large quantity of magic before?"

"Not like this." The scrawny man studied him intently, snorted in disgust, and turned again. "We're almost there."

They continued, and Romeo stuck his hands casually in his pockets. *When a whole batch of wolfsbane wears off and you're in the middle of the worst dark magicals' secret hideout. No big deal.* He took a few more seconds to be sure his guide wouldn't turn to shoot him any more dirty looks, then quickly pulled a handful of squashed purple flowers from his pocket and shoved them into his mouth.

Frank grunted behind him.

"What?" The leader spun again and stared at them like he had something better to do than lead an esteemed guest to a Black Heron werewolf pack.

His larger cohort opened his mouth and pointed to it.

"Did you bring a little snack with you, wolf?" The rat-faced man's huge nostrils flared to even larger proportions.

Romeo swallowed without even chewing and hoped the wolfsbane would get rid of his magical allergy as quickly that way. "Nope. I am hungry, though. Ravenous, actually. Do you guys have a mess hall or something? Oh. Maybe you have to wait for the dinner bell, huh? Yeah, it seems like that kinda place."

The man's eyes twitched before he shook his head and turned to move down the hall. "Shut up, already. We're almost there."

He clicked his tongue. "That's not very nice."

That didn't get any response from the magical leading him forward other than two clenched fists and shoulders that inched their way up on either side of his scrawny neck.

And if he's that pissed off by not doing anything, it means he can't. That's good to know.

Their little procession stopped abruptly a few minutes later, and the leader of his two escorts turned toward the wall. "Where is it?"

"Uh..." Romeo glanced around the hall that was even darker now and frowned. "Are you sure you didn't get lost? Seriously, I wouldn't blame you. This place is huge, but... uh, there's nothing here."

The man hissed an irritated sigh through his teeth and ran his hand along the smooth stone wall. After a moment, he stopped and pressed a piece of wall that looked the same as all the other pieces, and it actually clicked into a little recessed button. A whole portion of the stone slid aside with a rumble, and he nodded through the gaping hole. "Get in there before I lose it."

"What's this?" The werewolf peered into the darkness and sniffed, trying not to step away again or make a face. *There are definitely other wolves in there. At least six.*

"This is where you're gonna spend as much time as it takes for that witch to figure out what's good for her—and you." His unwilling guide pointed forcefully toward the open doorway. "Go."

"Okay. Sure." He stepped toward the dark entrance, then paused to look at the magicals who were only too glad to be rid of him. "Does anyone have a flashlight or something?"

Frank grunted and stepped toward him, towering over the werewolf by at least half a foot. His expression still didn't change, but he leaned closer and closer over him until Romeo nodded and raised a hand in front of his chest.

"I got it, okay. I simply thought I'd ask. Thanks for the escort, guys." He gave them a sloppy salute, mainly to see the annoyance flare in the scrawny man's beady little eyes again, then turned and stepped into the open section of wall.

It was dark enough that he moved slowly for the first few feet. The wall rumbled behind him again as soon as he was clear of it, and he stood there without moving, waiting for the echoing boom that signaled he was officially imprisoned inside a wall with no lights.

So where's the pack?

He slid his feet carefully in front of him across the uneven floor until his boot struck something solid. His hands knocked against what felt like a wooden door. "Maybe this was only the airlock." He slipped into a shift but only enough to see what was right in front of him and his vision pushed the darkness aside. It was definitely a door, but there was no handle, no lock, and absolutely nothing else in the four-foot box he'd been directed into.

A shout came from the other side of the door, followed by a few laughs. With a deep breath, he steeled himself to meet an entire pack with allegiance to the Black Heron and knocked loudly.

The laughter stopped. He waited for the appropriate amount of time it would take anyone to open a door before he knocked again.

The door jerked open with a loud creak and pulled

slowly all the way to reveal the quarters of the Black Heron's wolf pack.

"Hey." Romeo glanced around the large main room and counted six other bodies standing or sitting, although another of them lay on the floor. "I wasn't sure how long I was gonna have to stand there."

A woman with bone-white hair in long braids down her back and obsidian skin stepped from behind the door and folded her arms to scrutinize him like all the other wolves were doing. They seemed to be waiting for him to do something first.

Okay, there are seven.

Romeo jumped from the doorway ledge and dropped the few feet to the floor of the room. "I'm new and don't know if I'll be staying long. They brought me here and told me to walk right on in, so—"

"Did you come in with that witch?" A man with a glass of whiskey in his hand tipped his head back and shook the mop of pitch-black hair out of his face.

Squinting, he tilted his head and kept his expression blank. "Which witch is that?"

"Don't be stupid, man." The werewolf sprawled on the floor in front of the minibar raised his hand from the rug, waved it, and let it drop again. "We know who you are."

"Great." He gave them all a tight, close-lipped smile and shoved his hands in his pockets again.

"You know what we're doing here, don't you?" The woman with the white braids stepped away from him and toward the minibar. She glanced over her shoulder to raise her eyebrows at him.

"You mean here as in this entire castle-thing, or here in this room behind a stone wall?" He shrugged. "I'd have thought they'd give you something with a view, at the very least. This feels more like you're locked up."

The man with the whiskey downed the rest of his drink with an impressive display of no reaction whatsoever and turned to slump into one of the armchairs. "This is more for the regular wolves who join and ship out. We gotta keep the ones like you away from all the other magic for a while, you know?"

"We don't need the dampening wards anymore." The woman with the white braids poured a very tall glass of gin, added nothing to it, and turned again, swirling her glass. "But the first place they gave us here kinda grew on us."

Romeo tried to hide his frown and glanced quickly at the other half of the pack who hadn't said a thing yet. "You don't need the wards."

"Naw, man." The wolf on the floor raised his hand off the rug again and snapped his fingers. A tongue of purple flame burst at the tip of his fingers and quivered there. "It takes a little time to build up an immunity, but eventually, it works out fine."

With a long, slow breath, he tore his gaze away from the werewolf who'd conjured magical fire and looked first at the whiskey drinker, then at the woman with her gin. "All of you?"

"Yep." The man's hand darted over the armrest of his chair toward the bar from which he summoned the entire bottle of whiskey. It streaked across the room and into his hand, then he lifted it toward the newcomer in a mocking toast. "All of us. You wanna know how?"

"Uh...not really. My guess is it's not exactly the most awesome experience."

"Don't knock it until you try it." The wolf on the floor chuckled, stopped, then pushed himself up quickly until he was seated on the rug. "How come you're simply standing there?"

"Is something wrong with standing?"

"No, but..." The guy twirled his hand vaguely as if searching for the word. "What I mean is, you're simply standing there. Magic and stuff, inside the wards..."

This guy has totally pickled his brain. Maybe all of them if they drink like this all the time.

"Chase is trying to ask you why you haven't reacted to any of our magic." A small, frighteningly thin woman seated in another armchair lowered her hand slowly from where she'd propped her cheek on it and pointed at Romeo. "Why it didn't cause you any problems. I'm asking too."

"Oh." He spread his arms. "I guess I stumbled onto my own tolerance."

"From that witch, huh?" the wolf with the gin added. "The one Carmichael's been waiting for?" She nodded at her packmate with the whiskey when he turned in the armchair to shoot her a look.

"That's what everyone thinks she can do?" He raised an eyebrow. "It seems like way too much work to find one witch when you guys have learned how to still be were-wolves and do tricks with someone else's magic."

"So you know where it came from." The werewolf lifted the bottle toward him again, then took a long gulp. Romeo wanted to shiver for the guy.

"Yeah. I know."

"There's plenty of it, you know." The woman stepped away from the minibar toward the wolf's armchair and raised one leg to sit on the armrest. She brushed her white braids back over her shoulders with the hand that wasn't holding her gin. "If you wanted to get in on it."

He snorted. "Nope. I've been a werewolf all my life and I'm not really looking to add anything to it. If it helped you guys with your self-identity problems, great."

The thin woman in the other armchair hissed a wry laugh. "Listen to him. The guy has no idea what he's talking about."

"Well lemme tell you something." The prone wolf pointed at him again from his place on the rug. "If you think you can barge in here all high and mighty, you shouldn't have come. I'm glad I did it, and nothing's gonna change my mind."

"Cool." Romeo shrugged and headed toward the minibar. The pack watched him with wary eyes. Even Chase turned, although he swayed a little on the rug and had to prop himself up with a hand. "Is this an open bar?"

"Make yourself at home." The other werewolf tipped the bottle again and took another long chug.

"Thanks." Romeo bent to open the mini-fridge and grabbed a bottle of beer. He could go ahead and drink with them, but he wasn't about to allow himself to get wasted while he waited for Lily to find him. Or whatever else happened instead. He pressed the bottle against the edge of the bar, popped the cap, and turned to face the pack. After a long swig of beer that emptied almost half the bottle, he leaned back against the bar. "Look. I didn't ask to be let in, warded walls or not. And I didn't come to try to change anyone's mind. I'm merely waiting until whatever needs to happen actually happens, and then you'll never see me again."

The entire werewolf pack stared at him. In the next second, all seven of them burst out laughing. The man with the whiskey threw his head back against the armchair and roared with laughter. The bottle dangled from his hand and spilled liquor all over the rug with a muffled splat. His packmate with the gin was bent over her lap and held her glass out to the side.

He merely smirked and let them have their fun. *They've totally lost it. They might have magic but it backfired in a huge way.* He drank more beer, and the pack continued to laugh for much longer than seemed normal until a flash of purple flame launched from the rug and struck the stone ceiling on the other side of the room.

The laughter cut off, and the skinny woman in the armchair uttered a low hiss.

Chase glared at the hole his stolen magic had carved into the stone, then squinted with glassy eyes. "That's what they all say at first."

He turned his head slowly to meet the newcomer's gaze, on the verge of going cross-eyed. Romeo shrugged.

"I guess I'm merely special." He tipped the beer back

again and ignored the pack's snickers and the still-electric tension in the air. *And I have an Optatus witch who's gonna stop all this way before any of you can try anything.*

FOURTEEN

"This—" Carmichael spread his arms wide and tipped his head back as if he were soaking up the sun and the crisp mountain air instead of standing in a dark stone chamber. "This is where everything happens, Lily."

The space definitely looked like an altar for dark magicals to practice their ritual sacrifices and perform the kind of magic most didn't even want to know existed. The manacles chained to the walls every three or four yards around the circular chamber, plus the metal clamps closed tightly around scrying orbs, iron daggers, and pendants on long, thick chains definitely added an extra torture-chamber vibe. Lily fought to keep her anger from over-taking her completely. *This is where they'll torture the extra magicals they bring in for the rest of their spell. Not if I have anything to say about it.*

"What do you think?" Greta turned toward her daughter with wide, glassy eyes, her smile only half-formed.

She shot her mom a look that said, "You know exactly what I think about this," but there was no expression of recognition in the woman's blue eyes. Only a vapid hope and the dull remnant of suffering existed in that gaze.

"Don't hold back, Lily." Carmichael turned and tilted his head as he studied her expression. "I want nothing but honesty from you."

I really doubt that, but okay. "I think it's gonna be really hard to convince me that all this is actually worth it. For anyone."

"Ah. I assume you're talking about our donors."

She almost choked on the euphemism. "Donors? You've abducted magicals all over the world to bring them here. I've seen it. And if they're not kidnapped, they're killed out in the street for every non-magical to see and their magic is stolen anyway."

The man smoothed his dark hair, brought a hand down to stroke his goatee, and nodded. "I see where some of this confusion is coming from. I regret that side of things. I'm sure that on your journey to us, you noticed a few wayward members of our organization who haven't looked quite...right."

"Yeah, a few." She folded her arms. "It's hard not to notice them when they're attacking me."

"Yes." Carmichael nodded and stepped farther into the chamber. On the left was a kind of parlor set away from the black stone table in the very center. It was completely separated from the manacles and the clamps and the various magical artifacts that were most likely almost as dangerous as the Varelos in the wrong hands. He crossed toward the four armchairs arranged in a circle around a low table and beckoned both Antony women to join him. "Please, have a seat." He lowered himself into one of the chairs and gestured toward the others.

Greta stood rigidly in front of the armchair opposite him and sat slowly and stiffly like she had an iron pole strapped to her back. A slow sigh escaped her, and she extended a hand to brush her fingers against her daughter's arm. "Go ahead and sit."

Lily studied her mom's blank expression and looked for any sign of the woman who'd given her all her intelligence and strength and magic. There was none. "No, I'm good right here."

I felt her still in there when she squeezed my hand. She has to still be her in there.

Carmichael ignored them both and continued to talk as if the young witch had called to schedule a meeting as a prospective participant in this wildly dangerous final spell of his. "We've worked toward this goal for quite some time, Lily. A decade, at least, if not longer, although the idea was formed and presented long before the real work began. When we started, word spread quickly of the success we had with the Transference. Do you know what that is?"

Greta gave no reaction at all to the mention of the Transference. Lily nodded. "I know what it is. That's why you took my mom in the first place."

"Yes!" His eyes widened and the white orb of glass lit up in the light beside his one good eye. "Greta's discovery of this artifact was an invaluable addition to what we were trying to do at the time—the last piece of the puzzle we were missing. At least, that's what we thought at the time. As it turns out, we still needed something more for the Transference to successfully do what we needed it to. We needed someone."

When he glanced pointedly at Greta and offered the woman in his custody a sickeningly sweet smile—like a proud father doting on a prodigy child—Lily's stomach tightened in too many knots. Her mom wore the same proud expression. *There's no way she fell for this.*

"You chose the wrong witch, then, didn't you?" She fought another wave of rage and despair at the same time.

"Not the wrong one, Lily." Greta extended her hand toward her daughter, but she couldn't bring herself to take it. "Only half of the whole. What we want to do can only be done with both of us standing side by side."

A tingle flared to life at the back of Lily's head. Without bringing it up on her own, one of the images she'd seen when she'd touched her mom's golden tree burst into her mind as if projected on a screen in front of her. It only lasted a second, but it was crystal-clear—Lily and Greta, standing together in the same black gowns, working as one in this ritual chamber. *That won't happen. We will not help them.*

With wide eyes, she stared at her mom and her nose stung as the precursor to tears she didn't want to show anyone now. The woman tilted her head and smiled. "It's always been you and me, sweets. It only makes sense that we'd be brought together again to do what must be done."

For a split second, the glassy haze across her mom's features vanished, and Lily saw the real Greta Antony beneath it. The realization struck the young witch force-fully in that moment.

These are more clues. The tree, the visions, everything she's telling me right now. She's still in there. She's showing me how to get us out of this.

Lily's heart thudded in her chest but she kept her composure and shook her head. It was time for her to spin the greatest lie of her life.

She turned toward Carmichael and seemingly ignored her mom's words. "That's what 'complete the circle' means, isn't it?"

The man chuckled and stroked his goatee again. "Your mom's told me so much about you, Lily. I think she under-valued your intelligence."

More false compliments. "Why do you need me?"

"There's something special about your mom." He gave Greta another one of those doting looks, which made Lily want to blast him in the face with an attack spell. "She found the Transference, of course, which gives her a certain level of our esteem in and of itself. Regrettably, it took longer than any of us would have liked to craft the spell that could use the Transference the way we wanted to. When we found Greta again, we wanted to gift her with the product of what her discovery provided for us. The transference of magic simply didn't...take with your mom. Whatever it is about her wouldn't accept the magic freely given by our donors."

"We still don't know why, sweets." Greta shook her head and stared at the table in the middle of the armchairs.

The Black Heron still doesn't know what we really are. Or at least that I'm an Optatus too.

"And when we'd exhausted all our options with bringing her into the fold of our society—enhanced magicals with the ability to use magic in any of its forms we chose—I realized that what is in her and prevents her from accepting the magic was exactly what we needed to power this Transference spell for all of us." Carmichael shrugged and brushed invisible dust off the sleeve of his smoking jacket. "We tried everything we knew to bring this about, Lily. Even Greta's own blood pulled from her and isolated into its most powerful state with the Transference itself. But that final ingredient in the blood is not complete without all of it. The last witch of Greta Antony's familial line."

"You, Lily." Greta extended her hand again, her glassy eyes wide and red-rimmed and pleading with her daughter. But she didn't use her nickname, and there was no second vision to go along with it.

Lily knew that was how she'd tell the difference between what Greta wanted her to know and what she wanted Carmichael to hear.

She huffed in contempt and glared at the leader of the Black Heron Society. "You need my blood."

"Maybe not." Carmichael shrugged and glanced at the old, worn book bound in black leather that rested on the table between them. "I know enough now about how the Transference works that I think we don't need anything more than you and your mom working together. The power in your bloodline, fully completed with the two of you, should be enough to complete this final step."

"You're saying all this like the final step will help the entire world." Lily shook her head. "I don't buy it. Not when what I've seen over the last few months is nothing but the Black Heron terrorizing magicals everywhere they go. The murdering and kidnapping and harming innocent people who have no idea that magic even exists."

The man nodded. "I can admit that, if we follow the trail for that mess all the way to the top, I'm responsible for it. But let me assure you, Lily, those Black Heron members you saw doing these things did not operate under any official sanction of mine or the Black Heron Society at large."

Lily swallowed and fought to keep the images of all the kidnapped, tortured, and murdered magicals she and Romeo had seen between there and Charleston and all the terror these people had unleashed because of it at bay. "If you're at the top, you should've been able to stop them."

"I thought so too." He steepled his fingers under his chin, closed his eyes, then opened them and pointed all ten fingertips at the young witch. "Let me make this perfectly clear, Lily. Those members of our organization—if they can even call themselves that—are a select few who have come to be...well, restless and reckless, quite honestly. When we perfected the use of the Transference your mom discovered, it allowed us to siphon abilities from our willing donors and imbue ourselves with different forms of magic. Many of our members offered themselves as well for the opportunity to be among the first in this new breed of magical. We had many successes, I might add. But success never comes without a few hiccups. Some might even call them failures."

"Or mutants."

His chuckle was sardonic. "Yes. That is the very real result of combining a new form of magic with an unstable subject. It made them greedy, you see. Impatient. And when we discovered that we did not have absolutely everything we needed from Greta when she came to us—"

"When you abducted her." She clenched her fists.

"Fair enough." Carmichael held her gaze and his one eye blazed with a sudden flare of determined irritation. They stared at each other for a few seconds before he tilted his head a fraction of an inch. "May I continue?"

She clenched her jaw and shrugged.

"When this faction within our organization got word that we did not have all the pieces, they decided it was much more worth their time and effort to try to do on their own what we as a whole could not. Those are the magicals you saw on your journey here. Those are the people who have used the process we created to take magic from others that was not freely given. That is not the way the Black Heron Society operates, Lily. Those...mutants, as you so aptly put it, are on their own now, as far as I'm concerned."

"I already know that much."

For the first time, he actually looked surprised. It was brief—merely a twitch in his eyes and a tiny flicker of confusion in his brow before it disappeared, but it was definitely there.

Now he's wondering if someone's spilled the beans on all their secrets. Lily fought to hide her satisfaction. "I saw it in a text. I had to chase off one of your members, and the guy left his phone behind."

Carmichael narrowed his eyes at her, then took a deep breath and tried to play it off like nothing in the world could bother him now. "I'll have to tell my members to be more careful with sensitive information."

"Yeah, that's probably a good idea."

The man leaned forward in his chair. "Do you understand what I've explained to you?"

"Sure. You're saying that everything I've seen of the Black Heron so far has only been the rebel magicals trying to play god with too much of other people's magic. And that the rest of you stick to the rules and only take the magic that's offered willingly."

"Do you believe it?"

She stared at him, hoping that would make him show more of his discomfort but he had obviously pulled himself back together behind a much stronger wall this time. "Not really, no. What I've seen didn't at all look like only a few members going against the grain. It was big. And you killed all of them outside your own front door."

"I didn't believe him, either," Greta added. She turned her head toward Lily but kept her gaze fixed on Carmichael. "Not at first, sweets."

This time, the image that came forward in Lily's mind wasn't one of the hundreds the golden tree had given her. It was her own memory—her mother chained to a dark stone wall by manacles that could have been any of these in this chamber and tortured with spells intended to draw her magic from her. *She never believed him.*

"And your mom has seen her error in fighting what no one will be able to stop. This isn't everything I have to show you, Lily. There's more that I think will really change your mind." Carmichael slapped his hands on his thighs and pushed himself to his feet. "I have someone else who's very much looked forward to speaking to you."

Greta stood slowly from the chair, still rigid and straight-backed. She didn't look at her daughter, her eyes trained on the man like a dog looks at her master. *It's all fake. Remember that.* Lily pushed her disgust back down and turned to see him raise his finger from a panel of glowing green buttons on the stone wall. He slid his hand into the inside of his smoking jacket and pulled a rock out, of all things. Casually, he turned it over and over in his hand, ignoring it completely as he gestured toward the chamber entrance.

She stayed where she was and scowled at the double doors to the ritual chamber, both of which Carmichael had flung wide open and left that way. They waited for a tense and silent few minutes before quick, light footsteps echoed toward them from the corridor beyond.

FIFTEEN

"I completely understand that you wouldn't take my word for it, Lily." Carmichael flashed her that disgustingly false smile again. "And it stands to reason that after what you've seen of your mom before both of you arrived, you might be a little hesitant to believe her too. But if you listen to Carol's story, I think you'll feel differently about what we're trying to achieve here."

A woman appeared in the chamber's entrance. She had to be in her late sixties or early seventies, her hair mostly white with a few short streaks of gray remaining. But she moved like she was twenty years younger with a confident optimism that felt completely out of place. The woman nodded at Carmichael with a warm smile, nodded at Greta standing beside him, and caught sight of Lily.

"Oh..." A grin lit up her features, and she stepped haltingly toward the girl like she couldn't believe what she was seeing. "Is this her?"

"It is." Carmichael raised an eyebrow at Lily and nodded.

"Finally." The woman reached her and held both hands out. Her eyes—one a glittering violet and the other a bright silver—shone with excitement and a few unshed tears. "My dear, I can't tell you how much of an honor it is to meet you in person. And to have you here with us."

She watched the woman with a small, contained smile. *What is this?* Greta gave no indication that something was wrong and of course, Carmichael was showing her what he wanted her to believe. "I'm sorry," she told the woman. "I'm not sure what you're talking about."

"That doesn't surprise me at all after what you've been through. My name's Carol." The woman's hands were both still extended toward her and she didn't lower them when the young witch didn't immediately respond.

"My name's Lily."

"Lily. That's a beautiful name. You are your mother's daughter through and through. I can see that." Carol took Lily's hand in both of hers anyway and almost crushed the life out of her fingers when she squeezed. She released the pressure and patted the back of her hand. "We have waited for some time to see the final results unfold, and now you're here. I want to thank you."

"Um..." She couldn't help the confused chuckle that escaped her. "Thank me for what?"

The woman released her hand and gestured toward the black stone altar in the center of the chamber. "With you here, we can finally complete what we set out to do. We can help so many others the way your mother helped me when she discovered the Transference seven years ago."

Lily gaped, utterly confused. Her mom stood immobile beside Carmichael, her hands clasped in front of her again. Greta looked up only briefly at the mention of her, then returned her gaze to the floor. "I still don't understand."

"Carol is one of the original founders of the Black Heron Society," Carmichael interjected. "And, more importantly, the catalyst for our search. The doctors gave her six more months to live."

"I'm...so sorry." She didn't know what to say to the woman whose mismatched eyes unnerved her more than they should have.

Carol continued to smile.

"That was a little over six years ago, Lily," he said.

"What?"

"It's true." The woman took a deep breath and nodded. "Only six months. I was ready to make my peace with it, but Carmichael would have nothing to do with it."

"And a few others," he added.

"Well, yes, but you headed the whole thing, didn't you?" With a wink in the man's direction, she returned her attention to Lily. "When your mother discovered the Transference, we knew we'd found our possible. My last hope. And it worked, Lily. Your mother found the one thing that could reverse the disease and enable me to live seven years longer than anyone thought I would. And possibly far longer than that, judging by how I feel this far along in my life."

My mom helped them do this? "Mom?"

Greta raised her gaze slowly toward her daughter. "There are two sides to every coin, sweets."

Another vision slipped into her mind—Carol standing at the altar in this room with three other magicals chained to the walls around her. They were all werewolves, clapped in the iron manacles Greta herself had been forced into for so many months. The woman was at the center of it all, casting a mini version of the magic-siphoning spell and both her eyes glowed the bright silver of a werewolf before a shift.

How does she know all this? Lily glanced at her mom, who'd returned to staring at the floor again like an obedient servant. *Listen to the clues, Lily. Pay attention. That tree did more than simply give me information.*

"So yes, Lily." Carol nodded vigorously. "I want to thank you. Because with you here, standing beside your mother and bringing our spell to fruition, you will be saving hundreds if not thousands of magicals from the same fate I escaped."

"Please don't thank me," she whispered.

"You have every right to know the truth, Lily." Carmichael stepped toward them and nodded. "We're not trying to hide anything from you here, but I'm sure you realize what a delicate situation this final spell will bring about once we complete it. We can't let the world know what we're trying to accomplish. There are too many people out there who would want to stop us or to have a say in how we do what we do. Which, I might add, we've perfected quite well over the last few years, merely not on the large scale we all envision."

Lily frowned at him, then asked Carol, "Who's magic did you take?"

"I'm sorry?"

"If the Transference spell saved your life with someone else's magic, who gave it to you?"

"Oh." She blinked profusely and uttered a small, muted chuckle. "A very dear friend."

"Who was perfectly willing to give of themselves so Carol could be free of her illness," Carmichael added.

"You weren't born a werewolf." Lily pointed briefly at her own eye to indicate Carol's perpetually silver iris beside the other of a softly glowing violet.

"No, Lily. I was born a witch." Her smile widened but it was stiff and now, the woman didn't blink at all.

"That's a really good friend, then. It must have been an extremely strong friendship, right? There aren't many werewolves anywhere who share personal things with witches—or anyone else, for that matter. Especially their magic." She gave the woman a genuinely warm smile—not from the idea of whoever Carol's friend had been but because she knew she'd caught these people in a corner.

Carmichael cleared his throat. "As I'm sure you've noticed, Lily, the Black Heron Society doesn't discriminate based on race. We have magicals of all kinds within our ranks. Warlocks, necromancers, fairies, and yes, even werewolves. Most of us are witches of one kind or another, but our eventual aims reach so much higher than the type of magic with which a person was born."

Lily cut her gaze toward the man and raised an eyebrow. "Clearly."

Behind him, her mom coughed a few times and took in a wheezing breath. "Excuse me."

Everyone turned to stare at her. Greta covered her mouth with a hand, cleared her throat, and stared stoically at the floor.

She knows. Don't smile.

"Thank you for your time, Carol." Carmichael met the hybrid witch's gaze and both sported smiles that looked like they'd been painted on statues.

"Of course." The witch laid a hand on Lily's shoulder and squeezed it in apparent gratitude. It felt like a warning. "It's an honor to have you here with us, Lily. I'm so glad you've decided to do the right thing and join us in this cause. I won't be the last to thank you. I can promise you that."

She smiled and nodded before the hybrid witch turned and stepped through the open doors of the ritual chamber. In the silence that followed, she stood there with her mom and Carmichael, the air hanging thick and tense between them before Carmichael sighed.

"She's a testament of strength and perseverance, Lily. A symbol for everything that can be achieved when great magical minds come together for the greater good."

"It sure looks like it." She stared through the entrance at the corridor's far wall even after Carol's echoing footsteps faded completely.

"I'd like to show you how this will all work." He held his arm out for Greta. Her mom didn't even hesitate before she linked her arm through his and stepped away with him.

Lily took one more glance at the hallway, then forced

herself to follow the man who wanted to convince her that this was all one giant work of philanthropy. The sight of her mom walking alongside him, her hand resting on his forearm as she held it gently, made her shiver. *Keep it together. Get as much info as you can, Lily.*

He stopped beside the first black granite pedestal against the chamber's circular wall. It held a clamp with a divining crystal grasped firmly in its center. When Lily stopped a few feet away, she noticed that a soft yellow glow emanated from the crystal and pulsed weakly every few seconds. "We've gathered some of the most powerful artifacts relative to their magical sources and the races most likely to be affected by each. This, of course, is a fairy crystal."

Staring at the artifact, Lily folded her arms and pretended to study it as if she'd stepped into an art gallery. "What's with the clamps?"

"Protection only." Carmichael gestured across the ritual chamber to indicate the other artifacts held on marble pedestals exactly like this one. "We can't afford to compromise these items during the spell. The amount of magic it takes to power even a smaller version—say the transference from only one magical to another—is enough to do serious damage if performed incorrectly. The nexus of power we'll create here, in this very room, is almost unimaginable. But we've taken certain precautions. These devices protect the artifacts, and the artifacts will protect us."

She wanted to laugh. *He thinks he has this all neatly planned.*

"Okay…" She nodded toward the chains bolted into the stone wall and the shackles at the end of them that lay empty and open on the floor. "What about those?"

"Yes." He pursed his lips and nodded. "Those do create a contradictory picture, don't they?"

Lily couldn't help but glance at her mom's wrists. Both were hidden by the long sleeves of the gown Greta wore, probably for that very reason. But she had the marks on her own wrists to prove that she'd find the identical thing on her mom's if she bothered to pull those sleeves up. "Those are used on prisoners."

"No, Lily." The man shook his head. "Not prisoners. I know I don't have to remind you that our magic donors are all perfectly willing to provide what we need—"

"Why are they so willing?"

The man blinked in surprise at the interruption like he'd assumed he'd made his point the first time she did it. "We pay them." His nostrils flared and he tried to smile again.

"It must be a hefty amount."

"It's enough for everyone who comes to us looking for a way out. Some of those people are magicals on the verge of death, Lily. Like Carol. Some merely wish to open their minds and their perspective with a taste of what it's like to hold the magic of a race so different from their own. Some suffer in other ways, and we can alleviate that suffering by paying them for their troubles."

She pressed her lips together. "Right."

"Now, please come take a look at this." He motioned toward the black marble altar in the center of the room and he led Greta in that direction while he stared at the woman's profile. "And I think I'll let your mother explain this next part to you."

Another shiver skittered down Lily's spine, but she approached the altar anyway. She didn't yet have all the pieces she would need to finish the rest of her plan. *Namely how I get Romeo and my mom out of here in one piece.*

With Carmichael and Greta on one side of the altar, she stopped on the other side and only came close enough to clearly see what was already laid out there. Her mom lifted one of the many vials of brown-tinted glass and turned it this way and that in her hands. As far as Lily could tell, the liquid inside the vial was clear. *It's probably not water. No. I saw that vial in the tree's visions too.*

"This is the key to performing this spell." The woman looked up from the vial and frowned at her daughter. "Except for you, of course."

The room fell silent again, and Carmichael patted Greta's hand on his arm before he released her. "Tell her what it's for."

"Every participant in the Transference spell will drink one vial of this potion, Lily. Including the two of us. This is to make the whole process much smoother for everyone. Much less...painful."

"So you'll anesthetize a whole group of magicals." Lily frowned at the dozens of vials placed carefully in three concentric circles on the altar. "Before they're supposed to cast a spell so powerful that those artifacts need to be bolted to granite."

Carmichael inclined his head and eyed Lily for a few seconds, his lips pursing repetitively as he searched for words. "It's not alcohol, Lily. It's not a drug. What your mom holds in her hand is more of a dampener on harmful side effects. It does not dull the mind, nor does it tamper with a magical's ability to perform."

"Like a local anesthetic."

"I prefer to think of it as more of a cleansing agent. Our biological systems will be cleared of any ability to feel the discomfort of the spell, ensuring that every other faculty is as sharp and crisp and free from distractions as possible."

Without waiting for either of them to continue the tense discussion, Greta returned the vial to its place in the outermost circle. She lowered her hand behind the large, glossy black bowl carved of obsidian in the center of the altar. In silence, she lifted a dagger carved from bone, oiled and sanded enough to gleam a bright white in the low light of such a dark room.

Lily managed not to flinch when another vision from among so many opened itself in her mind. The tree had shown her that dagger passing hands, tipped with a bright-red drop of blood. There was no blood on the knife now, but the whole thing made her intuition about this place even stronger. None of it was good.

"The ritual knife." Her mother laid the dagger flat across the palms of both hands and raised it over the black bowl. "This is where your blood will complete the circle, Lily."

The young witch studied her mom's eyes, which were focused on the knife. "My blood."

"And mine. It's all part of the process, sweets. If we want to finish what we started."

There it was again—Greta calling her sweets. So there was another clue in there somewhere. *We literally have to give them our blood before we get out of here. Why?*

"Greta and I have spoken a great deal about this part of the spell." Carmichael stretched to take the dagger from Greta's open palms before he returned it to its place on the other side of the bowl where Lily couldn't see it. "She thinks it will cause you far more distress than anything else here. That you have a certain...constitutional weakness when it comes to blades."

Lily looked at him and tried to appear as nervous as possible. *I definitely didn't expect that. Okay, so I need to play the game.* "Well, I'm not gonna simply stand here and let someone cut me with that thing if that's what you're wondering."

"Hmm. I suppose that would be a little nerve-wracking, wouldn't it? Don't worry. It's only a few drops of blood in a few dozen potions. Nothing you won't recover from." Carmichael smiled and raised a hand to swipe a few strands of Greta's blonde hair away from her face. He tucked more of it behind her ear and the woman merely stared at the black stone of the altar and didn't so much as flinch.

"Your mom has really come a long way in the last few days, Lily. When she realized what we're really trying to do, when she came around and changed her old ways of thinking about us, about all of this..."

He gestured with his other hand at the ritual chamber,

his gaze still focused on Greta's profile. "Let's say I know she has the best intentions for your wellbeing and how to make this the best experience for you that it possibly can be. Which is why I agreed to let her oversee the creation of the potions the two of you will take at the start of the ceremony."

"What?" She couldn't have held that one back if she'd wanted to, and she didn't have enough time to know what she wanted—or what she thought.

"Does that surprise you?" He lowered his hand again and fixed her with a bright, amused gaze. His smile was probably meant to be reassuring and lighthearted, but it was one of a predator about to pounce. The rock in his hand turned over and over as he studied her.

"I..." Lily gaped at the man and caught another glance of Greta standing beside the table, unmoving and staring at the black table in a daze. "I didn't expect you to let her oversee anything. Look at her."

His chuckle came through his nose in triumphant little bursts. "I see a beautiful woman, Lily. A powerful witch. A magical who's dedicated herself to the greater good of our kind. And by that, of course, I mean the magical world at large. Not everyone can be here to receive the gifts of the Transference spell at the beginning, but we get to show them what it means to come together as one. To have access to all magic, in all forms, and to use it as we see fit. I trust Greta enough to allow her this one small responsibility. After all, she led you right to me."

Her heart fluttered. *He knows. About her raven totem, all the clues she left, and everything she did to protect me and show me how to get here. What's she doing?* Her mouth ran dry, and she knew she had to get a firm hold of what came out of her mouth next—and how she used it.

"What's he talking about?" She stared at her mom and Greta's unflinching devotion. Lily hoped that was devotion to this incredibly convincing act on her mom's part and not actual devotion to the man's insanity. "Mom?"

"I wanted you here as much as he did," Greta muttered. "We need you, Lily. Everyone here needs the magic only you can give this spell. Everyone who will come to us in the future, asking for it. This is all for them."

Shaking her head, Lily took a step away from the table. *Play the game.* "What did he do to you?"

"Carmichael gave me exactly what I needed to see the truth." Greta's eyelids fluttered, although her gaze didn't move from its focus on the altar. "He gave me only what I deserved."

The man hummed in satisfaction and continued to play with the rock in his hand, almost as if he'd forgotten it was there, in the first place. "It shouldn't be nearly as hard for you to come to the same realizations, Lily. Not with your mom here to show you how it's done. How much this will mean to her."

"What it means to her?" Lily glanced from one to the other. "I haven't seen her in six months, and she barely knew I was there when we stepped into that room. She doesn't know what anything means to her. Because of you."

Greta's eyebrows flickered together. "Lily..."

Taking a deep breath, Carmichael closed his eyes and

licked his lips. For a moment, he was completely still, the perfect image of composure—except for the stupid rock in his hand. "Greta, you haven't finished showing your daughter the final step of the process."

The woman gave a demure, trembling nod. The muscles of her throat clenched and faded again as she fought an unseen struggle within herself.

I really hope that's part of the act too. If it's not, I don't know how I'll save her.

SIXTEEN

With an open hand, Greta gestured toward the obsidian bowl on the altar. It was wide and shallow, like the chip bowl Romeo's dad had kept filled in the center of his kitchen table when they were kids. Lily forced that image aside.

"This," Greta said, "is the Weiyan—the conjunction of all the magic drawn from our donors. It will be collected here and redistributed when the spell is finished."

"Redistributed." Lily scoffed. "To all the Black Heron members, you mean."

"Not all of them." Carmichael ran his finger around the edge of the pristine, shining bowl. "My most trusted first, of course. As well as myself. And yes, before you ask, I have experienced this spell on a much smaller scale so I know what to expect. Which is why I've put so much thought into how we'll perform the much larger Transference spell with as little danger as possible for everyone involved."

She definitely didn't miss the much more obvious twitch of his eyelids around the white glass orb where his other eye used to be. *I bet that's how he lost it.* She had to look away from him, and her attention focused on the manacles and chains bolted to the walls around the chamber. "There are only ten."

"Ten what?"

"Ten sets of prisoner's chains." Her nostrils flared when she said it. "Do you really expect me to believe that you'll draw magic from ten people to fuel this spell and give enough to your few dozen members? That any of you will be satisfied with only a fraction of someone else's magic?"

He sent her the predatory smile again and lowered his head slightly to look at her from beneath darkened brows. "No. I don't expect you to believe that. And none of us would be satisfied with the magic that remains in the equation you so eloquently described. Our donors, the ten who will be stationed around us when it's time, will only power the Transference spell. The magic itself will come from somewhere else entirely."

"Where?" Her mind immediately went to the temple at Ichacál—the place that was supposed to be a haven for magicals seeking sanctuary from the outside world. Countless magicals had been locked in cages beneath the temple's foundations, their magic siphoned out of them by the Wisemen posing as hosts and healers and guides while they worked with the Black Heron Society instead.

"That will be revealed to you the next time you and I

stand in this room together. Which we will, Lily. One way or another." His gaze trailed slowly across the altar and over all the items laid out there in preparation for the spell she was willing to do anything to stop.

"This is the best thing for all of us, Lily." Greta finally looked up from the table and met her daughter's gaze. She stepped closer to the man and placed one hand on his shoulder like they were old friends. "It's time for you to stand with us to do what must be done."

Her other hand went slowly to Carmichael's, in which the rock turned over and over with a soft whisper of stone on skin. She focused on his hand and cupped the bottom of it gently. "It's time for you to stand with me, sweets, and help me to accomplish what I can't do without you."

Lily knew exactly where she'd seen that image before —two hands, arranged exactly like this, with the rock in constant motion in one of them. That part of the golden tree's vision came to her again so powerfully, she had to take a step back and shake her head. When it cleared, her mom looked up quickly from the rock to stare intently into her eyes.

That's it. That's what we need.

Carmichael stopped the reflexive action of his hand and frowned at Greta. By now, though, she'd returned her focus to his hand again, as if she'd fall on one knee in front of him at any minute and beg him for some kind of blessing. The man clenched his hand around the rock and shoved it quickly into the inside pocket of his smoking jacket. He grasped the woman's hand and guided her around the side of the table until they stood in front of Lily with nothing else between them. "Now that you've seen the process, now that you know everything there is to know, there's only one thing left to decide."

She knew he expected her to give him an answer without being prompted, but she didn't intend to give him the satisfaction of doing that simply to move things along to please him.

He stared at her for a moment and narrowed his eyes before he forced himself to say it out loud. "Will you stand beside your mother and the Black Heron Society to bring the Transference spell to life and fulfill this calling?"

She didn't look away from him and instead, focused on the one gleaming eye and the white orb of glass beside it. Lily had a feeling that somehow, the false eye could still see. "No."

"Lily!" Greta yanked her hand out of her captor's and flung herself at her daughter. "Lily, you have to do this."

It took everything she had not to break down and beg her mother to tell her the truth—to throw off the mask and quit pretending that she actually believed any of this. But that wouldn't get her where she needed to go. *Let them think the night has already come.*

"No, I don't."

"No. No, please." The woman took her daughter by the shoulders and gave her arms a little squeeze. It completely contradicted the force of her desperation that appeared to border on panic. "Lily, listen to me. This spell has to happen and it can't happen without you. We need you."

"Stop saying that!" She spread her arms and shoved her mom's hands off her shoulders. "You're not like these people, Mom. Whatever he's done to you, I'm not buying it."

"Then do it for me." Her lower lip trembled, and Lily's heart broke. "I need you."

"I can't." She shook her head and stepped away, fighting against everything in her heart that told her to simply give in so she wouldn't have to see Greta Antony like this. But her head told her—all the visions and these last few clues told her—that this was what she needed to do. "You're not yourself, Mom. I don't know what happened but you would never agree to something like this. I won't, either. This is crazy." *And I feel crazy too, now.*

"So that's your decision, then." Carmichael nodded without threats and without looking even remotely disappointed. In fact, he looked far more excited now than he had about anything in this whole stupid charade.

"Yeah." Lily glared at him. "That's my decision. I'm not gonna help you make a group of super-powered hybrids so you can continue to steal more magic and do whatever you want to whoever gets in your way."

"No. Lily. Don't say that." Greta shuffled toward her again and reached out with grasping hands in an attempt to bring her daughter under control. "If you hold a mirror up to this whole thing, sweets, I promise, you'll see the truth behind it."

Her mouth almost fell open. Not at her mom's words strung so closely together that they were barely under-

standable but because of the brief flicker of Greta's gaze—
to the silver-framed mirror charm on the chain around her
daughter's neck. *The necklace...*

"Like I said, I wanted you to be perfectly honest with
me." Carmichael moved past her toward the panel on the
wall with the buttons and all the blinking lights. "It looks
like we get to do this your way now."

Greta fell to her knees in front of her daughter with a
shrieking sob. "Carmichael, don't! Let me talk to her alone.
I can make her understand. I will. Please, I'm begging
you."

"Your daughter has a mind of her own, Greta." The
man said it in a singsong voice as he pressed a button on
the panel. "I admire that and I'll enjoy breaking her of that
minor obstacle."

"Lily!" Scrambling on her knees, the woman managed
to grab her daughter's hand and clasped it firmly in hers—
but not firmly enough for all those tears. They were real
enough, streaming down her cheeks, and made Lily feel
heartless and cruel for simply standing there.

This isn't Mom. None of this is real. Play the game.

"Do the right thing, sweets. We don't have a choice."
Her mom gave her hand another little squeeze and looked
at her. Despite the words and the tears and the groveling,
Greta's eyes were perfectly clear. There was so much
power there behind them and so much strength. She
nodded once in the second that Carmichael's back was
turned, and that told Lily everything she needed to know.

The young witch fought back her own sob. *There she*

is. I have to keep going now. She squeezed her mom's hand in return and did one of the hardest things she could do in that moment.

"I'm sorry." It was a whisper, although she made sure to make it loud enough for Carmichael to hear. Then, she pulled her hand from her mother's grasp and stepped away from the woman who was falling apart on the floor in front of her.

"I didn't want it to come to this, Lily." Carmichael stood at the entrance to the ritual chamber now, his hands clasped behind his back. "And I only hope, for your sake, that you're not nearly as strong as your mother seems to think you are."

Lily spun away from her mom. "What?"

Two women in black robes entered the chamber and had already fixed the young witch with warlocks' red, glowing eyes. They had the palest skin of any other warlocks she had encountered, which was many more now than it had been six months before. Their bleached white hair hung like silk over their shoulders, and she only knew they were women because of the way the robes fell over their bodies.

"What's going on?" Lily summoned her sparking red attack spell and let it crackle on her fingertips. *I can't fight my way out of this without showing exactly what I am. Let them think the night has already come. I can do that but it's gonna hurt.*

The warlocks clasped their hands together beneath the overly long sleeves of their robes and raised them to chest height. Two twin spheres of red magic bloomed within the circles of their arms, and a low chanting of incomprehensible words echoed through the chamber.

"This is your way, isn't it?" Carmichael gestured toward the warlocks. "Go ahead. Show them how it's done."

She snorted at the man. "If I had my way, I wouldn't still be here."

"Well, we can't all get what we want, can we?" He nodded at the warlocks, who didn't pay any attention to him anyway. "But I will get what I want from you, Lily. It's merely a matter of how long you're willing to fight."

The warlocks' blood magic flashed between their arms. A red streak darted toward her with incredible speed. She stepped back and deflected it with a warded shield that directed the warlock's attack into the wall mere feet from one of the marble pedestals.

Carmichael sucked in a sharp breath. "Make it quick."

One of the attackers stopped her chanting and lunged forward. A red, shimmering net burst from her hand and launched toward Lily. The young witch ducked and rolled across the floor, then released her own retaliatory spell. It struck the attacking warlock low in the thigh, and the woman shrieked but she didn't stop. A low wail rose from her throat, which quickly dissolved into a hiss. Black specks spewed from her mouth and swarmed toward her target, filling the air with a high-pitched whine and thick static. Lily focused her spells on trying to deflect the swarm, whatever it was.

A few of the black specks made it past her warded

shields and settled on her skin. "What the—" They burned like embers off a roaring fire, and the minute she jerked away in pain, the swarm moved faster.

The forceful blast of energy she delivered next did nothing to keep the attack at bay so she turned to the blue fire. It was almost impossible to put out and definitely not with water. It struck the second warlock—who still chanted with the red orb between her arms—at the hem of her robes. The woman merely glanced at the blue fire licking at her garment, hissed something a little louder than her chanting, and the spell extinguished.

Okay, they're a little harder to take care of than the others. They wouldn't be if I could use my Optatus magic, but that's off-limits. She gasped again when a few more black specks landed on the back of her neck and generated searing pain.

"Don't fight it!" Greta screamed from in front of the altar.

"Of course I'm going to fight it!" The black swarm whirled faster and faster around her, closed in from every direction, and ejected a few specks at a time to burn her in all the worst places. Now, she couldn't even see her target, and the static in the air around her make her neck prickle and her hair lift around her head. *Nice touch, though, Mom.*

She launched another streak of red sparks and they exploded against something too solid to be a warlock.

"I said quick!" Carmichael roared.

The warlocks' chanting suddenly stopped. In the same instant, the swarm of searing, blood-magic particles collapsed inward around Lily. The pain was overwhelming, and she uttered an involuntary scream. She thought she heard her mom shriek in the chamber too, but that might have been the echoes of her own voice before everything went dark.

SEVENTEEN

"Wolfsbane? Are you serious?" In the Black Heron's needlessly warded werewolf den, the whiskey-drinking wolf stared at Romeo, his mouth contorted in a mixture of disgust and disappointment. He had learned the man's real name—Tobias—and the dark-skinned woman was called Athena.

"I swear." Romeo lifted his second beer toward the guy and grinned. "I'd love to prove it but it turns out, I ate the last of what I brought with me."

I don't care how chummy they've become. I won't say a word about Rosalia's pot of always blooming wolfsbane in the Winnie.

Chase, still lying on the floor, responded with a startling guffaw that lifted his head and half his back with the force of it. "That's really gonna blow when it stops working and you're still here."

"Yeah, well, it could be worse."

"How's that?" Athena gazed at him from beneath

hooded lids and a small, doubtful smile pulling at the corners of her mouth.

"Oh, I don't know. Something like being teleported with an entire village of witches through Mexican mountains for a couple of hundred miles—vehicles and supplies included." He took another sip of his beer and smacked his lips. "Hypothetically speaking."

"It sounds like you spend considerable time with witches." It was the first thing the hybrid werewolf seated on the other side of the minibar had said since Romeo had entered this room. The others had introduced him as Oscar, but he'd had his back turned toward the rest of the group the whole time, apparently more interested in reading the book in his hand than in entertaining an outsider wolf who still didn't know if he was a guest or a prisoner.

"I guess I do, yeah." He waited for him to turn but it never happened.

"I wouldn't go around telling people that."

"Huh." He glanced at the others who'd deigned to talk to him. "Why's that?"

Oscar stretched in the chair and his booted feet slid along the rug beneath him before he crossed one over the other again. "It makes it sound like you sold out. Like whatever pack you came from didn't want you anymore, so maybe you tried to make a new one with witches."

Chase snorted a laugh. "Witches don't run in packs."

No one decided to comment on his insight into the obvious.

"I really don't care what it sounds like." Without a face

to focus on, Romeo frowned at the back of Oscar's chair. "And I don't have to explain anything."

"Then you'll keep running."

Athena stuck her thumb out toward Oscar's chair and tilted her head. She'd had enough gin by now that it was amazing she could even sit straight anymore, but her head did sink incredibly low toward her shoulder. "He only talks when he thinks he has something important to say. It never is, though."

Romeo raised the bottle to his lips again to avoid the awkwardness of not having anything to say to that. *This is the weirdest pack I've ever seen.* He swallowed while he considered his next words. "Okay, so did all of you arrive here together? As a pack?"

Athena and Tobias glanced at each other before she finally stood from where she'd sat halfway on his armrest. She moved to the opposite wall beside the door leading out into the hallway and leaned against it. "No."

He waited for any of the others to speak, but no one did. "That's what you are now, though, right? You guys made it all the way out here to the middle of nowhere, simply to be a part of the Black Heron Society. And without any real packs already established, you said screw the system and screw the rules, we'll make our own."

Tobias sniffed and shrugged. The whiskey bottle in his hand was only about a quarter full now. "Somethin' like that."

"No, it's not something like that." Oscar slammed his book shut and tossed it onto the floor beside the armchair. "You come in here acting like you don't care about anything, asking about how we got to be who and what and where we are." The armchair creaked beneath him as he pushed slowly to his feet.

"I'm only tryin' to make friendly conversation, man." Romeo raised his beer bottle at the back of the man's head. "That's all it is."

"But it sounds like you're trying to stick your hand in where it doesn't belong." The man straightened all the way and paused.

Okay. The dude's way taller than me. I didn't expect that. Romeo drained the rest of his beer and walked toward the minibar to give himself something to do. He wouldn't have any more beer but at least he could be a decent guest and stick his trash somewhere out of the way. "I'll put my hands in my pockets if it makes you feel better."

He heard the werewolf turn to face him and smelled the musky, electric scent of an alpha preparing for a fight.

"I won't feel better until you're out of here."

"Look, man, I'm not trying to challenge you or anybody else. I don't even want this. Not that you don't have a nice place or any—" He turned from the minibar and might have dropped the bottle if he hadn't already put it down. "Wow. You're tall. Where are you from?"

Oscar towered at least half a foot over him, probably more. His white-blond hair fell a little over his eyes, matched by the thick, six-inch beard dangling beneath his chin.

"We guessed Norway," Tobias interjected. "Viking werewolf fits well, huh?"

Romeo managed to curb his astonishment. "Yep. That would have probably been my first guess too."

The other man took another step toward him and bared his teeth in a grimace of irritation. "I want you to stop talking. Got it?"

"Sure." He shrugged and glanced around the main room of the pack's quarters. "But...what else is there to do down here?"

"Only five minutes," Chase said from the floor, slurring his words. "Give him five minutes of silence, then he's back to his old gentle self. Trust me."

"I'd like to." He stared at the pack's alpha and swallowed uncomfortably. "I gotta admit, though, I don't really trust anyone in this place."

Oscar didn't blink and didn't look away from the werewolf he wanted so badly to intimidate. A low growl rose from his throat.

Great. I talked myself into making them think I'm comfortable enough to be here. Now it looks like I talked myself into a challenge I really don't want.

"Okay." He raised both hands and took a step back. "This is not what I was trying to do."

"I don't—"

A low buzz sounded behind him, then another from the other side of the room. A few more followed in different places, and the last came from Oscar's pants. Romeo froze and watched the pack's alpha reach into the back pocket of his jeans to pull a cell phone out.

"Is something important happening?" When he

glanced at the other werewolves, they were all looking at their phones too, which happened to be identical.

Chase glanced at his, scoffed, and tossed it onto the rug beside his head. The others all looked at the newcomer with wide eyes.

Oscar's, though, narrowed into a squint, and he returned the phone to his pocket. His smile, when it finally appeared, made him look sick more than anything else.

"You feelin' okay?" Romeo took another step back and glanced around the room when Tobias stood from his chair and the tiny woman named Rebecca rose from the couch. The two other werewolves in the pack—whose names he hadn't heard once—had been too focused on their chess game in the corner to involve themselves in anything until now. They stood too and moved slowly toward the half-circle of chairs in the center of the room and the lone were-wolf who'd recently joined them.

"Yeah, actually." The alpha uttered a low chuckle and his huge chest moved up and down. "It looks like we finally know what to do with you."

"Really?" Romeo backed away from the minibar to put a few feet between them, but the other wolves were closing in on him now too. "That came through in the text, huh? Anyone wanna tell me what it said?"

The only answer he received was another low growl from Oscar as the man's eyes flashed a bright silver. He grinned and raised an open hand. A ball of crackling blue energy burst to life in his palm.

The other hybrid werewolves followed with their own

warning growls of varied enthusiasm, and each one of them summoned a spell as they stepped toward him.

"Something tells me you guys aren't simply showing off anymore."

Chase finally stood from the floor and stumbled around a little before he summoned the purple flames in his hand again. He burped, grimaced, and joined the others. "Nice knowin' ya, Roger." He flipped his hand toward their target, and the purple fire followed.

Romeo ducked, and the spell spun into the wall behind him. He crouched low and growled in return as his eyes flashed silver when he prepared to shift. "I didn't do anything."

"But you will." The crackling blue energy in Oscar's palm doubled in size with a hissing crack.

He snarled and let his wolf come forward for the full shift. Unbelievably, he wasn't fast enough to escape Oscar's spell—one a werewolf should never have been able to cast. The blue energy caught him in the chest, and an agonizing jolt of electricity seared through his entire body. It reversed his shift and he crumpled to twitch and convulse under the shock. His jaws were clenched together so tightly, he thought he could feel his teeth breaking, but he couldn't make his body do anything.

The Black Heron's werewolf pack moved in around him, accompanied by a few muted chuckles as he completely lost his hearing. The jolt of Oscar's spell lasted much longer than his ability to stay conscious.

EIGHTEEN

When Lily woke, her body was on fire. The moan that escaped her didn't sound like her own voice, and she barely managed to open her eyes enough to glance at her legs curled toward her chest. *I'm not really on fire. It only feels like it.*

It took her longer than she wanted to be able to move again, and even longer than that to push herself up off the cold stone floor. Her head pounded like someone had dropped a boulder on it, and she grunted when her back and her head thumped against the wall behind her at the same time. *None of the recovery from training with Mom could top this headache. What was that spell?*

She grimaced and tried to look around. The room felt like it was spinning, but all she could see was blackness. When she tried to slide her leg under her, a metallic clink filled the air, and her leg wouldn't move as far as she wanted. "Seriously?"

Scowling, she stretched a hand out to confirm with her fingers the iron manacle she already knew was there. That small movement of her arm made the chains of the one around her wrist repeat the same metallic clink. The burning all over her skin faded quickly and now, she felt everything else—iron cuffs on both wrists and ankles, the chill of the cold, dank air, her bare feet scraping on the stone, and the tickle of something sticky that had dried on her temple and the side of her face.

"Oh, good. I'm chained to a wall with dried blood on my head and probably a concussion." She took a deep breath, which made her head throb a little harder, and exhaled slowly. "But this is exactly where I want to be, isn't it?"

She leaned her head carefully against the wall and tried to focus on her memories of the ritual chamber. *That was well-played, Mom. The tree. The clues. Vials and knives, and Carmichael's pet rock.*

"And the mirror," she whispered. The ridiculously short chains these people kept her on jerked her hand back when she tried to touch the mirror charm at her throat. With a grunt, she hunched over and was able to reach it. *It's still there. That's part of it too. The Varelos even said it was important and that I'd use its magic with Romeo. Once within and once without.*

"I'm sorry." She said it to her mom and she said it to Romeo too. There was no way Carmichael hadn't punished at least one of them, if not both, for her refusal to buy the man's lies. "I'll get us out of this but I have to make it look real."

A heavy metal bolt slid somewhere in front of her, and she straightened again to rest her back and head against the wall. With a low groan, a door opened. The light spilling in from the hallway lit up the irrationally small space in which Carmichael had stowed his newest prisoner.

A box. They put me in a stone box.

Lily waited for whoever it was on the other side of the door to step in with her and do their worst. He didn't make her wait long.

A short man with a perpetual grimace of disgust stepped into the doorway, his features darkened by the light shining behind him. He propped himself up with both hands on the sides of the doorframe and leaned forward a little. "Look at that. You know, there's something vaguely familiar about what I see."

"Yeah, I recognize your ugly face, too." She forced herself not to look away, although the light in the hallway seemed to grow brighter by the second. *It's probably only the little bump on my head.* The thought made her snort.

"I really wouldn't laugh if I were you." The man lowered his hands and took a single small step into the cell. There wasn't room for much more than that. "Your mom laughed too, all chained up like that. And she finally broke."

She couldn't actually tell him how wrong he was, so she settled for, "I'm not my mom."

"No truer words." He scrutinized her with evident disdain, and she finally remembered why she recognized him. "You look exactly like her. Especially like this. I'm willin' to bet you don't hold out half as long as she did."

"You're the one in charge of breaking me, then, huh?" She licked her lips and steeled herself for what she knew was coming. *An Optatus witch has to want something. It won't be hard to want this to be quick.*

"For now, yeah." He shook out his hands and stared impassively at her.

"Good luck. I saw how much you failed with my mom. This isn't gonna look good for you when you fail to break her daughter, too, who knows so much less and has barely grown into her own magic."

"Yeah, you're her kid, all right." The society member cleared his throat and cracked his knuckles. "You'll stop talking. Eventually."

Lily smirked. "Are you stalling? I don't think Carmichael sent you in here only to—"

A wiry, writhing cord of magic erupted from the man's open palms and struck her in the chest. The stone box around her illuminated with the violent streaks of flashing white that flared from his attack.

Her head cracked painfully against the wall behind her, but she hardly felt it. The only thing she could feel was the agony in her chest that seemed to burn all the way through her and into her to search every particle of her being for what it wanted—what it didn't get from Greta Antony and would never get from the witch's daughter.

Every muscle in her body contracted at once, and the Black Heron's go-to man for trying to siphon an Optatus' magic—without knowing it for what it was—leaned forward into his spell. The pain shoved a high, shrieking whine into her head, or maybe it was her own voice screaming. She bucked beneath the attack, unable to move or to do anything but endure. Exactly like her mom.

After what felt like an eternity, the witch in the doorway retracted his spell. The black cord sputtered, and Lily sagged against the chains behind her. It didn't matter that the manacles bit into her wrists when she leaned forward. All she wanted was to press her forehead against the cool stone floor so she could stop the burning and come back to herself.

Both of them were breathing heavily.

Yeah, like it was as hard for him. She surprised herself when a soft, low chuckle escaped her at the thought.

The man sniffed and wiped the sweat from his forehead with his arm. "I swear, both of you are completely insane."

"Yeah, I had a good time too." A sharp bark of a laugh escaped her and disturbed a cloud of dust with her face pressed against the floor. "I'm lookin' forward to next time." A grunt of disgust was the man's only reply. When she looked up again, wanting to see his face and the disappointment there, the heavy iron door was already halfway closed again. It settled into place against the stone wall with a bang and plunged the young witch into complete darkness again.

"I get it," Lily whispered. "I totally get it now. I won't be in here doing this nearly as long as you, but I know how you did it." Her entire body ached, every muscle limp after what she'd endured. Despite the pain and the exhaustion, she continued to laugh against the stone floor of her prison. "It's almost over, and they think they're only getting started."

NINETEEN

It felt like a game without any real rules or end. The Black Heron Society sent their masters of magical torture to Lily's few feet of personal space repeatedly to try to break her. Every time, she endured the spells intended to take her magic from her. After every failure, the witch who'd made his or her best attempt left in a huff while she laughed them out into the hallway.

They brought neither food nor water and no one came for anything but to send the searing coils of dark magic burrowing into her in an effort to break through. Each session lasted a little longer than the one before it, but for the indeterminable lengths of time between, she had more and more time to practice the magic Greta had passed down to her.

An Optatus witch gets her power from desire. She gets it from what she wants.

That was her mantra now, and it strengthened her against the hours of agony. She left her body when the society members opened the door, and there was nothing they could do to shove her back into it while they cast their spells again and again. Better yet, it seemed that they didn't even know.

"You look awful," one man said whom she hadn't seen before. She barely saw any of them.

"Really? I thought a lack of food and sleep was supposed to do wonders for a girl's figure. You should start a blog for beauty tips."

"What?"

"I said—"

The pain began again. When it was finished and another unsatisfied torturer locked her in the dark cell again, she knew she was almost there. "Only a little longer. We're almost done."

The next time the door opened—which could have been a few minutes or more than a few hours—Lily could immediately sense that something had changed. The biggest giveaway was the sound of more than one pair of footsteps moving around outside. *Mr Grimace steps lightly. Clown Nose likes to stamp. Ring Lady tiptoes everywhere. Who is it this time?*

One pair of footsteps didn't really sound like footsteps at all.

"Did you bring a friend with you?" she croaked. Her time there had done that to her. Perhaps it was all the screaming. "It sounds like he's not feeling very well with all that shuffling. You should have that checked out."

"Yeah, we did that." It was Clown Face this time—a huge necromancer hybrid with fairy magic, as far as she could tell, and a nose like a sweaty, bulbous strawberry. "Whether things get better or worse for him is all up to you now."

She lifted her head from where she'd rested it against the wall and squinted into the light. "Romeo?"

"Hey..." Clown Nose held him up by the collar of his shirt. The werewolf swayed and dragged his feet, barely able to stand on his own. "Nice place they set you up with, Lil. How you doin' in here?"

One of his eyes was swollen shut, purple and bruised above a split lip and copious smears of blood everywhere like he'd been tossed around in it for a while. The rest of him didn't look much better, but in the bright hallway light, she couldn't see anything bleeding freely, at least not right now. His good eye swiveled toward her but he could barely keep it open.

He's barely holding on.

"It's not too bad actually." The last word broke into a harsh, wheezing sound. "I think you'd like it."

Romeo chuckled. "We can compare notes later."

Clown Nose gave him a rough shake and had to pick him up again when his knees buckled. "This is on you, witch. We found ourselves running a little low on were-wolf magic. Everyone seems to want some. Hell, I'd take it. Carmichael thought you might wanna see up close and personal what the spell looks like when it's powered by someone you know."

The werewolf snorted. "He never asked me."

The huge hybrid released the collar to slap him across the face with the back of his hand. He grunted and slumped again, and the Black Heron member had to grasp two fistfuls of his shirt to pull him back to his feet.

"Stop it," Lily muttered.

Romeo spat on the ground in front of him. Even in the low light, there was clearly blood in it. "It's okay, Lil. I think this big guy's trying to be all threatening and stuff."

His captor scowled but didn't move to strike him again, knowing what a valuable bargaining chip he was for the witch chained up in the tiny cell. "Or you can give up this tough-girl act and help Carmichael with the rest of the Transference. Stand with us, as it were, and the werewolf gets to keep all his own pure wolfiness to himself."

Her friend looked like he wanted to say something else marginally witty, given the circumstances, but let his mouth snap shut in silence.

Lily leaned forward against the chains around her wrists. "That's what Carmichael said?"

"Yep. I talked to him about half an hour ago before I picked this piece up off the floor."

Romeo's head sank toward his chest for a moment before he raised it and settled his dizzy, unfocused gaze on her. Very slowly, he shook his head.

"Remember what I told you?" Lily nodded at him and hoped he was lucid enough to hear her and understand what she meant.

"Yeah, I don't believe a word out of this joker's mouth, either." He might have winked at her but it merely looked like blink with his other eye swollen shut.

Good. He remembers.

"Huh." The man glanced suspiciously from once to the

other, one held in his grasp and the other chained to a stone wall. "I would have thought you'd take less time to make a decision."

"I can't."

"Sure you can, witch. It's a simple yes or no." He shook Romeo by the collar again. "Help us out on your own, or your friend gets to help us with an extra boost of werewolf."

"I mean I can't agree to that." She swallowed and couldn't break away from the werewolf's gaze, even though it wandered a little given his one un-swollen eye.

The Black Heron member burst out laughing. "I honestly didn't expect that answer. Do you think you hit your head one too many times?"

"I'm sorry," she whispered and ignoring the giant completely.

Romeo stopped swaying enough while his captor held him up to stare intently at her and offer a nod of understanding. "I'll be fine, Lil. I trust you."

"Both of you have totally lost it." The man snorted, shook his head, and jerked the werewolf back away from Lily's cell. "I guess we have our answer then, huh, wolf?"

"Romeo, whatever happens," Lily shouted, "don't forget what I—"

The heavy iron door slammed into place again and plunged her into darkness again. She felt in her bones that it was almost the last time.

The next Black Heron member who opened the door was none other than Carol.

"Oh, look at you." There was a confusing mixture of

both sympathy and disgust in her voice. "I do wish you'd taken the opportunities presented to you from the very beginning, Lily. It would have made this whole thing so much less...messy than it's become."

Lily swayed where she sat and raised her head. She'd almost fallen asleep for the first time since they'd thrown her in there, which would have been the first time she'd slept in four days—plus however long she'd been in this stone box. "Messy."

"Quite." The witch's nose wrinkled and she stepped forward into the cell. "We can help you clean this whole thing up, though. If you take this incredible offer and do for us what you were meant to do for everyone."

She could barely see the woman's extended hand as her eyes couldn't quite focus on anything, even with the bright light from the hallway. "They weren't really your friends, were they?"

"Who?"

"The werewolves. All four of them whose magic you took at the same time. At the altar."

The cell fell deathly quiet for a moment, punctuated only by Lily's slow, ragged breath. *That's all I hear anyway when they leave me alone in here.*

Carol drew a sharp breath. "Where did you get that idea?"

She shrugged or at least thought she did.

"A little birdie told me." *A big black raven totem, actually.* The thought made her chuckle. *How did none of these people catch on to that one, Mom?*

"I don't think this is very funny, Lily." Carol crouched

in front of her and unwittingly displayed her spryness powered by werewolf magic—the same that had healed her disease, whatever it was. "You should take this seriously."

"You're right." She opened her eyes long enough to meet the hybrid's silver-and-violet gaze. It held the hopeful satisfaction she wanted to see before she got to tear it down again. "This is seriously the worst attempt I've ever seen at trying to get someone to trust you. I'm chained to the wall, Carol."

The woman scowled and pushed abruptly out of her crouch in one smooth, quick movement. "And that's where you'll stay until you can come to your senses, Lily. How long that will take is up to you. Me? I can walk around this building at my own whim."

Lily snorted. "Go ahead, then. I can't stop you. Seriously."

Her unintended play on Carol's seriousness brought another round of dry, cracking laughter bubbling from her throat. It cut off abruptly when the hybrid witch blasted her with the cord of dark magic. Black and white and flecks of red poured from the woman's hands into Lily's chest.

The young witch jerked against the force of it, unable to move until it was finished.

She was vaguely aware of her cheek impacting against the cold stone floor at the same time that the iron door slammed shut again. Her right arm, chained to the wall, twisted awkwardly behind her back but she didn't care. *It turns out stone makes a good pillow under the right conditions. Besides, it looks like I'm finally gonna get some sleep.*

TWENTY

Lily dreamt of the High Seat's black stone walls, although these were cracked and splintered and on the verge of crumbling into ruin. She watched the Black Heron's stronghold from somewhere above it as the center fortress caved in on itself and the outer walls avalanched into destruction.

"Don't forget to take my hand."

From where she floated high above the destruction, Lily turned and saw her mom beside her wearing the stupid emerald-green gown.

Greta nodded and extended her hand toward her daughter. *"I won't leave you again, sweets. But you have to take my hand. It's time."*

When she felt another hand in hers, she looked to her other side to see Romeo beside her too, their fingers firmly intertwined. She reached for her mom, studying Greta's confident, reassuring smile. The second she touched her fingers, a loud crack split through the air, and the rest of the Black Heron's High Seat in the middle of the Sahara imploded.

She jolted awake to the painfully bright light spilling through the open door to her cell. Part of her thought she was still dreaming because this time, no one stood in the doorway. "Worst dream ever," she muttered.

"I imagine your mom thought something similar, too." Carmichael stepped into the open doorway and blocked out enough light that her pounding headache eased a little. "I tend to think that when reality feels like a dream, we've finally stumbled upon the truth."

This time, she had no witty comment or ongoing joke running in her head that she could use to infuriate the society members who attempted to break her. *He wanted to see for himself what kind of progress I've made. I guess it's time now. Here we go.*

"Lily."

A heavy sigh seemed a suitable response.

"Look at me."

Lily didn't have to fake the heaviness of her head or her drooping eyelids when she craned her neck from where she slouched and met Carmichael's gaze.

"There. That's better." The man stepped into her cell and squatted in front of her like Carol had. Only with him, it didn't seem like it was for show. He was getting down to business. "Now, I wanted to have a little chat with you."

Her head swiveled as she tried to hold his gaze. *I'm exhausted, hungry, disgusting, and beat up. I don't have to be more convincing than that.*

"You've been in here long enough, don't you think?"

"Mm-hmm." The reply could have been mistaken for nothing more than a groan. She probably could have nodded more convincingly, but she wasn't willing to expend that much energy and besides, it added to the effect she wanted.

"Good." Carmichael stroked his goatee and examined her. "Those cuffs look painful, Lily. I'd like to finally get you out of them, but I need something from you first."

Her eyes widened. *This really is it.*

"I need to hear you say it."

Her lips parted, and she released a heavy sigh. "I...want..."

He nodded and watched her mouth, leaning forward as if that would coax her into continuing.

"I want to..." She stared at the collar of his smoking jacket. "Perform the spell."

Although her voice broke on the last word, it was perfectly audible to them both.

The leader of the Black Heron Society smiled grimly and nodded as if he understood the pain and the hopelessness in which he truly thought she now existed. "I know you do. I've always known. And now we have the truth, don't we?"

Lily meant to say yes, but all that came out was a short whimper. *Even better.*

"They say the truth will set you free, don't they? It would seem you will embody that quite literally." With a self-righteous little chuckle, he flicked his fingers at her. A yellow spark ignited at his fingertips and traveled along the chains, and all four manacles released. They clattered to the stone floor with a metallic clink.

The young witch remained where she was, curled in as close to the fetal position as she had been able to manage when the short chains had restrained her arms. The hand that had rested over the top of her hips slid forward now that it was free and thumped to the floor with a smack. Aside from that, she didn't move.

"There. Let's clean you up, put a good meal in you, and let you rest on a real bed. How does that sound?"

Despite the fact that she was completely lucid and completely aware of her intentions and the fact that she'd chosen to make it look like Carmichael had won, Lily began to shiver there on the floor. *Wow. No wonder Mom was so convincing. They made it way too easy.*

"Okay. Easy, now." He guided her gently by the shoulders to a seated position, nodded, and leaned forward to hold her gaze. "Look at me, Lily. Focus on me, and I'll help you out of this place. I can only imagine how awful it's been for you."

The laugh that escaped her sounded so much like a sob bursting from her cracked lips that she surprised herself with it.

"All right. It's okay." He continued to nod and smile like a grandmother taking a crying child's hand patiently and leading her to the table for a whole plate of cookies. "Come on."

Lily's legs hardly had enough strength to stand and she wobbled as much as Romeo had when he had been dragged in for a visit. *Whatever they did to him, he's okay. If*

they actually did anything, seeing as Carmichael the benev-
olent was so sure this would happen.

When she stood fully upright, her incredibly twisted captor turned savior pulled her against him for a hug. "I've got you, Lily. Everything will be okay. The worst of it is behind you. I promise."

The young witch sagged against him, mainly because she would have crumpled and fallen if she didn't have some kind of support. Her cheek smooshed up against the velvet-lined collar of his smoking jacket and her arms hung limp at his sides. He smelled like jasmine of all things. *Mom really pulled it off and didn't even flinch when he touched her. It turns out it's actually possible.*

A snort escaped her, and her chest wracked with silent laughter. Carmichael smoothed his hand over her matted hair in a soothing motion.

"Let it go. Soon, you'll be free of all this. Purified, you understand? Without anything to distract you from standing beside your mom and doing what you were born to do."

Not the way you think, Mikey.

"You're ready." Standing there with her full weight pressed against him, Carmichael snapped his fingers. The cell darkened as the huge, expressionless man who'd held Romeo back in the study however long ago ducked to enter. The leader eased her slowly away from him and into the hulking society member's arms.

Without a sound, the silent giant carried her like a sleeping child out of her prison and through the halls of the High Seat. Lily couldn't stop her head from falling back over his arm, and her hand dangled and swayed with each of his steps through the corridor.

This is only the beginning. She closed her eyes and felt every muscle in her body relax into complete nothingness. *The night is here.*

TWENTY-ONE

The huge mute Carmichael used as a pack animal took Lily to her new room. It was definitely not another cell and, draped in silks of bright colors and filled with twinkling lanterns lit by magical flames, looked like it belonged in a Middle-eastern palace. A massive bed stood against the far wall, also draped in silk from the banister frame around the four posts. There were too many pillows stacked on top of it to leave any room for an actual body but she didn't get to sleep. Not yet.

When the man placed her on a rounded settee beside the fireplace, she simply sat there, her head resting back against the cushions. As soon as he left, two women in black robes entered her room. One of them was the warlock who'd blasted her with the searing swarm of black specks in the ritual chamber.

Her eyes widened as the woman approached and stretched a hand out to help her to her feet.

"You have nothing to fear now, love." The warlock

nodded and the other women joined her to help her off the settee. "You've done the hard work and now, it's only smooth sailing from here. You'll be treated like a queen, you know that?"

These people are seriously messed up. She let the women do as they wanted and stared blankly at the empty fireplace.

They undressed her quickly and tossed her old clothes in a pile beside the entrance to the room. One woman reached toward the silver-framed mirror hung on the chain around her neck, and Lily forced her arm up to place her hand on the charm. "Please," she croaked.

The black-robed society members glanced at each other. "You can't wear anything from before during the ceremony."

"I'll...take it off before." She forced herself to meet the woman's gaze with dull, lifeless eyes. "Let me wear it until then."

With a sigh, the woman brushed her hand aside. "Let me see."

She was sure they wouldn't find the magic in the mirror charm. The artifact didn't give off even a trace of magic until it was actually used and even then, the reversal spell it cast left no residual footprint.

Finally, the woman lowered her hand from the charm and nodded. "All right."

Through the entire process—being stripped naked, led to a bath of steaming water in the connected bathroom, helped into it to be washed and soaped and scrubbed like a child—Lily didn't say a word. The women who helped her in and out of the tub, brushed her hair, and dried her didn't bother to start a conversation. That wasn't what they were there for.

Look at this. I have my own handmaidens and a private room nicer than the one I had in Mom's apartment. I should've gotten here sooner. A half-hiccupping laugh escaped her.

"Sorry." The society member who pulled the emerald-green gown over her head and jerked the bottom of it over her hips looked up quickly and raised her eyebrows. "I didn't know you were ticklish."

"She's many things no one knew before now, isn't she?" The warlock smirked at her companion. "As docile as she was bullheaded."

"The best qanas are always the hardest to break."

Both women snickered and led her to the settee. She sat obediently on the opulent cushions, and they took their places behind her.

"What's a qana?" Lily stared at the fireplace as her hair was brushed again.

"You are. And your mum." The warlock ran her fingers through her hair at the scalp and began to braid it. "There were more of you long ago when magicals weren't so scattered all over the place and so hard to lead."

"We'll fix that soon," the other woman added and returned to the settee with a tray of dazzling black jewels. "Now that you stand with the Black Heron."

"This is the beginning of something very big. You should understand that, at the very least, before the Transference. And you should be proud."

Lily let a smile flicker at the corner of her mouth. "I am."

The warlock finished braiding her hair in silence, and when she stepped back, the other black-robed woman walked in an agonizingly slow circle around Lily. She paused every few seconds to twist one of the black jewels into her blonde hair until Lily was sure her head was weighed down by half a pound of rocks.

Finally, the woman stepped away to get a better look at the human doll she'd dressed. "Perfect."

The warlock stepped beside her and nodded. "That looks exactly like I imagined. Better, even."

"Will Carmichael like it?" Lily gazed at them with the biggest puppy-dog eyes she could muster. She didn't even have to plan that part. *It's so easy.*

The women glanced at each other and offered her pitying smiles. "Of course."

The warlock bent in front of her and patted her hand. "It's natural for you to want his approval, love. But you're not doing this only for him. It's for all of us."

"I know." Her lips twitched in another sad, tired, void-like smile.

"Good. Marcus brought you something to eat." The warlock gestured to the small table with two chairs against the wall. "It doesn't look like much, but it's enough for what you need. Especially after you've gone so long without."

The other woman gave her a final careful scrutiny. "Can you stand?"

"Yes."

"You have a little time to yourself now before everything's ready, so rest. Think about what you're about to do. You'll have someone to help you every step of the way. If you need anything, that button will call someone."

Lily glanced at the panel on the wall beside the door, which had only one shiny silver button in the center. She nodded slowly and felt very much like a doll now and equally as stiff. "Thank you."

The warlock nodded toward the door, and both women left her without another word or glance. She steeled herself for the boom of a heavy door locking her inside again, but this one only closed with a soft click. Silence descended and she was completely alone, clean, dressed, pampered, and not okay with any of it.

But I have to be. We're almost there.

It took her a few attempts to stand but she propped herself up against the back and waited for her legs to stop shaking. "Yep. Exactly like a baby."

Her first few steps were stumbling attempts across the room, especially in the long gown that made her feel ridiculous. They hadn't given her any shoes.

Lily finally made it to the table and lowered herself stiffly into the chair facing the door. The tray held two peeled and quartered clementines, a few thick slices of cold ham, a wedge of cheese, two biscuits, and a small cup of soup that reminded her of the vegetable stew her grandma had made her when she was a kid.

"After all that, no one made me a sandwich." She smirked and reached first for the silver pitcher and the glass to fill it to the brim with water. "I guess that doesn't exactly fit the whole guest-in-a-castle vibe they have going on."

She drank two glasses of water before she started on the meal, and she didn't stop until even the crumbs from the biscuits were gone. Reeling from a full belly and the warmth of the bath and the fact that the stone box she'd gotten to know so well was now far behind her—if not that far below her—she stood and headed to the bed. It took a little more work than she wanted to swipe half the ridiculous amount of pillows off the comforter and onto the floor. But when she finally crawled up onto the huge mattress almost twice the size as her mom's California King in Charleston, nothing else mattered.

TWENTY-TWO

"Lily."

She stirred in her sleep, recognized the voice, but was unable to immediately remember who it belonged to.

"Hey." A hand brushed her hair gently away from her cheek, then settled on her shoulder and gave her a gentle nudge. It was warm through the fabric of her gown. "Wake up, Lil."

She jolted on the bed and pushed herself up so quickly it made her head pound.

"Woah, woah. It's only me."

"Romeo." With a sigh of relief, she flung her arms around him and held him tighter than seemed possible. *He's okay. And this will be the hardest part.* When she finally pulled away, there were tears in her eyes, which would only make this seem that much more real. "Are you okay?"

"Uh... I think so." He slid his hands down her arms

until he grabbed both of hers. "I'm still trying to figure that part out."

She studied his green eyes flecked with gold. He looked so much better than the last time she'd seen him, but there was something different. Not in his eyes but in the entire way he carried himself like he thought he would break anything he touched. "Did they—"

"Yeah. They did."

"I'm so sorry. I couldn't... I don't know what I was thinking."

He wrinkled his nose and let out a confused little chuckle. "Sure you did, Lil. Everything you said before we—"

"Shh." She pressed her hand over his lips and stared at him. "We shouldn't talk about anything...before. I don't want to. This is all that matters now. Starting over right here."

Romeo snorted. "What?"

She glanced quickly at the panel with the silver button beside the door. *Please pick up on that, Romeo. They're listening. They have to be if they let him in here.*

He glanced over his shoulder and searched the room. "I don't get it."

"You will. I want to explain everything, but I..." She squeezed his hand. "I don't know how yet. Only that this is where I'm supposed to be. With my mom."

"Well, yeah. When we get her out of here."

Lily shook her head and wished she could speak directly into his mind. As far as she knew, that kind of connection was only possible for magicals with telepathy and Optatus witches. Romeo wasn't either of those. "Romeo, I'm staying."

"You're what?" He jerked his hand out of hers and dropped it into his lap, staring at her as they sat so close to each other on the huge bed.

"I'm staying. I have to. I'll perform the Transference with my mom and with everyone else who'll be a part of it. We'll both probably stay here after that, too. Carmichael says—"

"Carmichael?" Romeo shook his head quickly, then slid off the bed and took a few steps back. "Are you kidding me?"

She couldn't say anything. *Please remember what I told you. No matter what I say or do, it's all a lie.*

"Lily, that's not what we came here to do."

"I was wrong, okay?" Lily sighed and held his gaze. "I... had time to think about it, obviously. And I realized the truth of what Carmichael's doing here. The Black Heron isn't a society of magicals bent on destruction, Romeo. They're building something wonderful. I can show you."

"Nope. Thanks." He scratched his head, turned in a tight, confused circle, and stopped to stare at her. "He got you too, didn't he? Exactly like your mom. Is this some kinda brainwashing thing, Lil? 'Cause I don't...this isn't you."

Lily spread her arms. "This is the most me that I've ever been. If you'd only listen to me, I can share it with you."

"Great. Yeah, that's great." He nodded and threw his arms out in frustration. "We come in here completely ready to follow through. Totally prepared, right?"

When he paused and held her gaze, it was long enough to be taken as an invitation for her to say something. *Or he's trying to tell me he gets it.*

"Then they pull us apart and now, neither one of us are who we were when we got here."

She frowned. "What do you mean?"

Romeo scratched his head again and shifted his weight but his gaze left her face to fall onto the bedspread. "Something happened. When they...tried to take my magic."

"Only tried?"

His expression a little fearful, he chewed on the inside of his cheek and raised an open hand. A few orange sparks crackled at his fingertips before a ball of bright white light flared in his palm. "I have weird magic, Lil."

Her jaw dropped. "You... That's..."

"I know." He stared at the ball in his hand, wiggled his fingers, and finally shook his hand until the spell retracted. "Turning it off is much harder than turning it on. Like I said, I'm still trying to understand...everything. I guess."

"What happened?" That was simply part of the act too, but she wanted to make sure he at least had some idea of what was going on.

"I have no clue." With a reluctant sigh, he returned to the bed and sat again a little closer to her than before. "Seriously, they had the whole thing set up with two other magicals who were supposed to take it from me. And... well, I ended up with this."

"That's not supposed to happen."

"Yeah, I realized that part out fairly quickly. Those witches were pissed." He smirked and his gaze roamed her face and her braided hair and all the glistening black stones twisted into it. "Do you have any idea what I did wrong?"

Lily had to fight so hard to keep from laughing. She could barely keep a straight face as it was. "You didn't do anything wrong. It looks like someone was simply lookin' out for ya."

"Maybe. It's a weird feeling, though, you know? Like something didn't want me to not be a werewolf anymore." His eye twitched into almost a wink.

Oh, my God. He gets it. Thank you.

She rubbed her hands down the soft fabric of the gown that was identical to her mom's. "I bet Carmichael could tell you what happened."

Romeo wrinkled his nose again but didn't repeat his last reaction. "Actually, he said he doesn't know what happened, either."

"You talked to him?"

"Yeah. He was the first person who stormed in when that spell backfired. I was, uh...kinda throwing spells around everywhere, I think. But when I somehow managed to make it all stop, the guy invited me back into his reliquary for a little chat."

"You mean that study?"

The werewolf smirked. "Yep. He calls it a reliquary, so I guess that's what it is."

They shared a private look of amusement at that.

Carmichael definitely had lofty illusions about himself and his position at the Black Heron's High Seat.

Lily shook her head. "And he doesn't know what happened?"

"Nope. He thinks I'm special, apparently. I guess he's never seen that spell backfire before, so he wants me to stick around."

A frown darkened her brow. "You should." *And he'd better realize I don't actually mean that.*

"I don't know, Lil." He gestured vaguely at their surroundings. "This whole place is...there's something not right, you know?"

She reached out and caught his hand again. "It's only change. A big change. That's what my mom and I are here for. You should come to the Transference."

He snorted. "You really do sound exactly like him."

"Well, he's right. I'm sure you can go if you want. Now that Carmichael thinks you're so...special."

"That's a no too. He already asked me to be there at the spell ceremony."

"Oh." She bit her lip. *This is gonna be tricky. He has to be there.* "What did you say?"

"I said I'd think about it, Lil. But I'm not sure I wanna be a part of it."

"Please come." There was no hint of falseness in her words now. He had to be at the Transference if everything she'd set in motion was to turn out the way she planned. *One from within, and once from without. The timing has to be perfect.*

"Why?"

Lily huffed out a surprised laugh. "What do you mean, why?"

"I want to hear it from you. Carmichael gave me this big ol' speech about what the Transference means for everyone. Bringing all the races together with all kinds of magic. Creating a new evolution of magicals to 'make things better.' Honestly, I don't see how it's any better." He spread his arms and glanced at his chest. "I'm some weird hybrid thing now, and I don't think there's a place for me with witches or werewolves anymore."

"That's the point." She squeezed his hand again and nodded. "That's what the Black Heron Society's for. And the more people we can bring into the Transference spell when we're able to do it again, the more we can tear the walls down. You'll see."

His grimace of distance wasn't a part of this whole charade, either but at least it fit what he was trying to show —if Carmichael really had eyes and ears on them. "Maybe. He did tell me that if I came and if I was there to see the spell and what happened afterward, I could leave if I still wanted to."

"You won't want to." *That feels so wrong to say.*

"He said that too." Romeo chuckled wryly. "I might show up. Maybe."

"And you'll change your mind. I know you will. You'll stay with us, and we can start over here." She took his other hand in hers now and wanted so badly to stop this stupid game and simply be real with him like they always had been.

"Yeah, I don't know. That's gonna be the hard part."

"Even if you were staying here for me?" It was a baited question—a trap for him if anything they'd said to each other was remotely true. *Trust me. Take the bait.*

He sucked in a deep breath and released it slowly. "I can't answer that question right now. And I don't wanna lie to you, Lil. I have no idea what's gonna happen."

"Okay," she whispered, slipped her hands out of his again, and set them in her lap. "You have to do what you have to do. I get that. So do I. I'm staying here with my mom."

"I don't—"

"Romeo." She raised a hand to stop him. "There's no changing my mind on that, so please don't try. I only hope that you're open to change yours. And in case you're not..." Her hands went to the clasp of the chain around her neck, where the silver-framed mirror charm had hung for months since she'd found it in that first box of clues Greta had left for her in an invisible cabin in Canada. She unclasped the necklace, pulled it away from her throat, and only had to catch his eye to get the point across.

"You don't have to do that, Lily."

"No, I don't. But I want to. I'm fairly sure they burned my clothes, which is fine. This is all I have left from...who I was before we got here. I knew I had to get rid of it, but now I know exactly where it's going."

Romeo cleared his throat. "You sound like you already know I won't change my mind. Is that what this is? Simply, 'Goodbye. Thanks for the road trip. Take my necklace?'"

"Only if that's what you want it to be." She held his

gaze and lifted the necklace a little higher. "But if being at the Transference doesn't convince you that this is where you belong, what I say right now won't matter. I'd rather give this to you than have no idea what happened to it."

He opened his mouth, closed it, and sighed. "If you're not leaving this place with me, Lil, I don't know if I want anything of yours."

"Then throw it away."

Slowly, with a confused frown and wide eyes, he leaned forward and let her clasp the chain around his neck. He swallowed, and it was loud enough for both of them to hear.

When she pulled away, she studied the mirror charm hanging below the collar of his shirt and gave it a little pat. "So. If you're still wearing this at the Transference, I guess I'll know that you've made the right choice."

Licking his lips, He glanced at the charm, then looked at her with a fierce intensity she didn't expect. "I still think you're making a big mistake, Lil. I hope you know the most powerful setbacks are the hardest to unravel."

Yes! He got it. This is what the Varelos was talking about. And we're actually gonna get away with it.

Lily held herself together. She couldn't reveal in her voice or her actions how glad she was that she'd gotten that message through to him. Instead, she cupped his face and the scruff growing there. "Then I hope you don't make the biggest mistake. It's all up to you now."

Romeo nodded, breathing heavily through his nose. "I guess so."

They sat there like that for a little longer, then he pressed his hand against hers on his cheek and finally pulled it away. "I should go, Lil. You probably have things to do before this whole thing starts."

She didn't, and they both knew it. *But it's too hard to keep sitting here talking in riddles like this. Being this fake.*

"Yeah. I think you probably should."

He leaned toward her on the bed and for a minute, she thought he would kiss her. It wouldn't have been that out of place—a potential last goodbye kiss. But instead, he grasped her shoulders and brought his lips to her cheek instead. He gave her shoulders a gentle squeeze and she closed her eyes.

"I remember," he whispered.

It was so soft, she barely heard it.

When he pulled away again, his mournful smile almost broke her heart. *The Black Heron made this easy. My mom and Romeo make it so much harder.*

Romeo slid off the bed and headed toward the entrance to her new room. When he stopped to open the door, he turned to look at her over his shoulder and gave her a tiny nod. Without a word, he slipped out into the hall and closed the door behind him with a soft click.

Lily remained where she was, tears swimming in her eyes. *I can't believe we actually did that. We're so close.* She buried her face in her hands so whoever was watching —and she was sure someone was definitely watching— wouldn't see the grin she couldn't hold back any longer.

It worked. The Varelos' spell protected him with the

mirror charm's magic. Once within and once without. That's how Romeo gets to use the mirror. I really hope he's paying attention because we only have one chance to get this right.

TWENTY-THREE

By the time Lily had her next visitor, she'd pulled herself completely together. Now, she merely had to maintain the act until the right moment. *Which might be a little hard, seeing as I didn't get that kind of visit from Mom.*

The man who'd knocked on her door was incredibly tall and thin with short-cropped hair with traces of gray at the temples and a pair of rimless glasses with thick lenses. He cleared his throat and seemed unable to look at her. "It's time."

"Good." She stood slowly from the settee in front of the empty fireplace and put on her best Black Heron special guest air. *It would've been easier to act like I own the place if I had shoes. Whoever said a pair of Louboutin stilettos didn't have a practical use is missing a whole lotta life experience.*

She approached the door and nodded as he stepped

aside to let her out into the hall. He closed the door behind him and inclined his head again. "If you'll follow me."

They moved silently through the halls of the High Seat's fortress, down the wide marble staircase she didn't remember climbing—even in the huge thug's arms—and along the various corridors. They didn't stop at the ritual chamber like she'd expected, but at Carmichael's reliquary instead.

The double doors were open already, and the tall man with glasses gestured for her to step inside. "Carmichael will come to call on you both in a few minutes." With another nod, he slipped away down the hall to carry out whatever other duties were required of him.

"Lily." Greta stood behind one of the desks next to the wall of bookshelves on the right, where she and two other magicals had whipped up a few more potions, apparently. "You look so beautiful."

Her daughter was momentarily stunned by the compliment. *It's the first time I've heard her comment on the way I look. While it doesn't fit the Greta Antony I know, that's not who we are right now, is it?* She recovered quickly and gave her mom a quick, fleeting smile. "So do you."

While her mother was still in the same gown she'd worn when Lily arrived, she looked far more composed now and definitely more sure of her purpose—which was the exact opposite of what everyone else there thought, except for Lily. The woman's hair had been decorated with the same black jewels twisted into her hair.

She does not look like my mom. I guess that's a good thing right now.

"Are you ready, sweets?"

Lily approached the desk, and the magicals apparently helping with the potions—those Carmichael had allowed the woman to oversee—continued to work as if no one else were in the room. "I'm ready."

"Good." The woman opened her arm for her to approach and ran a hand down the smooth fabric of her daughter's sleeve exactly like her own. "This is what we were discussing...before. With Carmichael. You remember our conversation, right?"

She frowned. "Why wouldn't I?"

Her mom opened her mouth, took a halting breath, and smiled. "Well, you spent a week on your own...reflecting."

It was impossible to miss the glance her mom's two Black Heron aides shared with each other. *A week? No wonder Romeo could summon a light orb that quickly.* "I haven't forgotten anything, Mom. I've merely learned so much more."

The smile Greta sent her was completely genuine and full of proud understanding. She grasped her wrist and gave it a little shake. "That's my girl. Now, while we still have a little time, I want to show you what Bernadette and Graham have made for us. Under my supervision, of course."

The man named Graham with only half of his left ear intact—and whose skin had an odd, wavering sheen to it—stared with wide eyes at the ingredients he was grinding with a mortar and pestle.

They all think she's an idiot now. Man, she's good.

"This is the special potion only for you and me, Lily. It

will provide a little extra to help purify our minds and focus our purpose. We're done with suffering through our old selves to reach our calling. Now, we get to climb higher." Greta thrust a hand into the air as if praying to a mystical deity in the sky. Then, she jerked her hand back down, batted her eyelashes, and sent her a self-conscious smile that lasted two seconds. "It's all very complicated. But as far as I know, that's the feverheart—"

"That's the bonekettle, ma'am." The thin fairy with sparkling purple hair in two braids down her back glanced at Greta and seemed to try very hard not to comment on the woman's stupidity. "This is the feverheart. You don't want to get the two of them confused."

"Would that make it taste funny, do you think?" Greta snorted in amusement.

"No. That would kill you."

"Oh." The woman grimaced, turned to shoot her daughter a look that said, 'Now I've been put in my place,' and clasped her hands together. "Well, that's why I'm only here to watch. That's good enough for me."

Lily almost burst out laughing. Her mom's friend Melissa Bore—the potions witch they'd found hiding in a werewolf den in Mexico—had told Lily only a few months before about Greta Antony's skill with potions. *She knows exactly what she's doing.*

The society members continued to grind ingredients and measure other liquids and worked in silence while the Antony women watched from a vantage point nearby. Then, Greta jumped a little. "Oh, Lily. There's a book about the Transference I thought you'd like to see before the ceremony. Will you get that and bring it over here? It's on the big desk in the back."

Bernadette and Graham glanced at each other again but kept working.

With a nod, she turned away from the desk and headed toward Carmichael's ridiculously large cherrywood desk beneath the stained-glass window of a flying black heron. The surface was pristinely organized with a carved wooden pen holder with individual slots, a pad of paper with the black heron in a circle embossed in the bottom left corner—she wanted to roll her eyes—and an empty, perfectly clean black mug in the center. "I don't see a book here."

"It must be in one of the drawers, then. Go ahead." Greta gave her daughter a dismissive wave and turned to watch the potions.

"I'd wait for Carmichael to come back, honestly." Bernadette stopped her work to look at Lily. "He's a little touchy about his things."

"Maybe with the rest of you," Greta said with a firm frown at the fairy. "But not with Lily. Go ahead, sweets. It's important."

She shrugged and grasped the handle of the first drawer. *What does she want me to see?*

"Please don't do that." Graham said it like someone who'd never had children trying to keep their patience with an ornery toddler. "It's not for you."

"Open the drawer." Greta merely nodded.

Lily pulled the drawer open, and a blue light flashed from the desk. The next thing she knew, she stood inside a bubble-shaped warded shield that emitted a low whine, which grew louder by the second. Bernadette and Graham both sent Greta a disgusted look, dropped what they were working on, and raced toward the desk. Lily simply stood where she was as if frozen in surprise but understood exactly what her mom was doing.

"I told you not to open that drawer," Graham lamented and fumbled under the lip of the narrow shelf built at thigh-level in the far wall. "Is that too much to ask?"

"Don't you ever speak to my daughter that way," the woman shouted.

The witch turned to glance at her and cringed. "Sorry. But we have so much work to do."

"Then fix whatever happened and finish that work."

Lily recognized only too well the stern fury her mother used now, which made it that much harder not to tell the society members they were really in for it if they didn't hurry. The warded dome's whine was almost painfully loud before it cut off abruptly and Graham removed his hand from beneath the narrow shelf. *Security alarm. Good to know.*

With a sigh, the man extended both hands toward the blue bubble around Lily and nodded at Bernadette, who'd stopped on the other side of it. She extended her hands too as they focused on the ward, and Lily caught the brief flick of her mom's fingers. A whole row of books behind the fairy toppled from the shelves with a rumbling clatter. One of them toppled a brass statue below it, and Bernadette whirled to look at the mess.

"What's taking so long?" Lily shouted.

"B?" Graham stared through the warded dome at his fellow society member.

In that moment, Greta thrust the long fabric of her sleeve over the mortar bowl Bernadette had used. With a hasty flick of her wrist, she sprinkled the final ingredient she'd saved for a disaster exactly like this one, perfectly manufactured to give her the opportunity she needed. Then, she stormed toward the desk and the society members who struggled to understand what had happened.

"You two are supposed to be the best," she spat.

"At potions," Graham shouted. "Ma'am."

Bernadette turned toward Lily, nodded, and held up a large, jagged dark-purple stone. "I think this fell and knocked everything down."

"Right." Her colleague frowned at the rock in her hand. "What a stupid bookend."

"Really? Do I have to show everyone around here how to do the simplest spells?" Greta tossed the sleeves of her gown up over her wrists and stretched her hand toward the dome. "This is ridiculous."

"Don't." Graham grasped her arm hastily, then realized what he'd done and quickly let go. "I'm sorry. Carmichael said you aren't allowed to practice any magic in here."

"Are you serious?" She scoffed. "What does he think I'll do?"

"It's so you can keep your strength up for the ceremony," Bernadette cut in quickly. "Resting, right? To be at your best."

Both society members nodded and looked grim and

entirely wary of what might happen if Greta Antony decided to ignore them.

"Well." She took a breath and tilted her head, her gaze roaming the blue dome around her daughter. "If Carmichael said that's what he wants..."

Turning her nose up, she spun toward the work desk again and glided across the floor, a dark magical queen in bare feet. Lily wanted so badly to pull the ward down herself, but that would've brought her a momentary satisfaction and much more work to put her façade in place after that. "Can you guys please get me out of this already?"

The two magicals cast their spell together—bright, flickering yellow strings of magic that wound themselves around the dome like so many snakes the width of a shoelace. When it was entirely covered, all the light vanished completely and Lily sighed.

"Thank you." She stepped out from behind the desk and didn't look at either of them, although she felt their irritation directed at her turned back.

"Oh. There it is." Greta chuckled and pointed at the low table between the massive leather couch and the armchairs on the rug. "I could have sworn I saw him put it away in the desk. Come here, Lily. We'll let Graham and Bernadette focus on the potions. I'm sure I don't need to watch them the whole time."

"You sure don't," he muttered. Everyone ignored him as he and the fairy returned to their station to finish.

Lily joined her mom in the center of the reliquary before they both moved toward the table in front of the couch. There, resting in the center of the table, was a huge grimoire bound in black leather. On the cover, of course, was a black heron with wings outstretched within a perfect circle, all of it embossed in gold. *Why am I not surprised?*

"Sit here with me." The older woman sat on the couch and patted the cushion beside her. She joined her, and they looked at each other before Greta took her daughter's hand. "You haven't had nearly as much time here as I have so you haven't had the chance to learn everything. There's not much time before we stand at that altar with everyone else, but I want you to know that I'll be there with you every step of the way. If you find yourself feeling lost, sweets, simply follow my lead, okay?"

She smiled at her mom and noted the lack of haziness in her eyes that had been there a week before. *Has it really been a whole week?* "Got it."

"Good. You've been through so much, Lily. Not only here, but before. I'm sure it was really confusing for you."

"I thought I knew what I was doing." That was as much as she could say without crossing the line and breaking their cover. *I can't believe all three of us are keeping this up on our own.*

"The important thing now is that you're here." Greta raised a hand toward Lily's hair, studied the black gems embedded in the braids, and settled for cupping her daughter's cheek. "I wouldn't have it any other way."

She can't say stuff like that right now and expect me to keep it together. She simply squeezed her mom's hand and lowered her gaze.

"Okay." The woman leaned forward and reached for

the Black Heron's grimoire on the table. "Now, let me show you what we—"

"If this isn't the picture of perfection, I don't know what is." Carmichael stood in the doorway to his reliquary, his hands clasped in front of him, and stared at the mother-daughter duo he'd so craftily brought under his wing. "Are you both ready to begin?"

TWENTY-FOUR

"We are." Greta stood from the couch with a broad smile and Lily did the same but without the smile.

"And the potions?" Carmichael raised an eyebrow at Graham and Bernadette who worked quickly on the bench beside the bookshelf.

"One more minute," the fairy replied.

"Make it quick." The man looked at the Antony witches again and gestured toward the space in front of him. "Come here. Let me have a look at the two of you in all your glory."

Lily followed her mom to stand where Carmichael had indicated. This time, when Greta faced the man who'd fought for months to break her down, she stood tall and straight, beaming at him as if she really did believe this was part of her destiny. Her daughter kept her reaction a little more understated. *I can lean on the guy after taking the chains off, but I don't think I can smile at him. Not like that.*

"Incredible." Carmichael shook his head and smirked as his gaze shifted from Greta to Lily and back again. "You two could be sisters."

"That's very kind of you." Her mother lowered her gaze, but the smile remained.

"It's the truth." The man stepped toward them and stopped a few inches away to bring his hand up under Greta's chin and lift her face to look at him. "I have the two most powerful magicals right here, standing in front of me, devoted to this vision and ready to do whatever it takes. I wouldn't have it any other way."

This echo of her mom's words made Lily's stomach curdle. Greta only smiled a little more enthusiastically and her blue eyes gleamed. Carmichael turned toward Lily and studied her from head to toe. "I can't tell you how happy it makes me to see you here, Lily. Like this."

She wanted to return his scrutiny but had to look away from him, afraid that her irritation would show in her eyes.

"No. Don't do that."

Her gaze flickered up to meet his. She didn't want to give him a reason to touch her face like he'd touched Greta's.

He raised his hand anyway and settled it not under her chin but against her cheek. The backs of his knuckles brushed softly from her cheekbone to the corner of her mouth. "You might not have the presence of mind for it at the ceremony, Lily, but just once before we start, I'd like to see you smile at me."

You've gotta be kidding me.

She focused her gaze intently on the white, glistening orb of his false eye and centered everything she had on the glassy surface so she wouldn't see a reaction there. Steeling herself, she forced a smile, which made her want to vomit.

"Ah." He lowered his hand and clasped his other wrist in front of him again. "That is so much better. Thank you."

Greta turned to look at her daughter, still smiling and wearing that mask of pure, almost ecstatic satisfaction. Seeing that look from her made it much easier for her to smile for real. *I can do this.*

Bernadette and Graham hurried toward them from the other side of the reliquary, each of them holding a vial of completed potion for the witches standing in front of their leader.

"Good." Carmichael gestured toward the door. "Go get those ready please."

Graham nodded, took the second vial from the fairy, and headed out into the hall without another word.

"Is there anything else?" Bernadette asked.

"No. You've done more than enough. The rest of the day is yours, Bernadette."

"Then you'll see me there."

"Excellent."

She turned toward the Anthony women, nodded briefly, and hurried out of the room.

"Now." The man smiled at his apparently doting witches—the only ones who could do what he needed—and held both arms out for them to take. "Let's go change the world."

Greta didn't hesitate to take his arm, and Lily forced herself not to flinch when the sleeve of her dress settled against the cold material of his thick black shirt. The man had dressed more for a funeral than a spell ceremony of immense and highly dangerous magic. *It might even be his funeral.*

Carmichael turned with them on his arms and led them out of his reliquary. "I've waited twenty years for this day. I had no idea it would turn out to look like this, escorting two gorgeous, powerful witches through the hallways I designed myself. It's funny how destiny works out, isn't it?"

He looked directly ahead, apparently no longer needing reassurances from either Lily or her mother that he was as fantastic as he'd convinced himself he was.

They moved through the hall of the High Seat and past all the open doors of the common rooms and specially designated areas. Everything was empty and quiet.

Way too quiet. Lily couldn't help peering into every open door and around every corner she could, looking for Romeo. *If I don't see him before we get there, it means we're still on the right track.*

She recognized the huge double doors into the ritual chamber even before Carmichael stopped them. They were closed, of course, waiting for the grand entrance of the Black Heron's leader and the witches in his possession. Every society member there thought that was exactly what Greta and Lily Antony were—Carmichael's possessions. His to control and guide through the massive spell that would do more damage than any of them could foresee.

But it won't. Lily turned to meet her mom's gaze under the proud jut of the man's chin between them. *Let's do this.*

The doors opened and swung into the hall. Carmichael stepped forward, and the witches walked with him. Lily almost choked when she saw what the ritual chamber had become.

There were more magicals crowded in this one room than she'd seen in the entire fortress of the High Seat, although that really wasn't saying much. A ring of two dozen society members, all in black robes, surrounded the huge, black stone altar in the center. The rest of the open space around them was crammed with as many Black Heron members as could fit, although they didn't wear the same robes as the chosen few. What little open space there was formed eleven paths that cut through the crowd. The first led from the entrance doors to the altar. The other ten also led to the altar, but when Lily saw where they ended, she had to focus instead on the slow, steady pace Carmichael set.

Put one foot in front of the other, Lily. And don't trip.

Ten magicals had already been shackled and chained to the walls around the room. In the overwhelming silence of the leader's arrival, a few whimpers and moans rose above the crowd of society members.

Willing donors don't sound like that. But she already knew that everything Carmichael had told her on her first day there was a lie. Soon enough, she and her mom would break it all down.

The trio stopped at the head of the altar, and he

lowered his arms until the two witches released him. Lily scanned the faces of the society members present, looking for Romeo. She almost passed over him completely. Someone had given him new clothes, all black, and she felt a little guilty for thinking that he looked exactly like one of them. She didn't hold his gaze for very long, but from the corner of her eye, she saw him surreptitiously touch the mirror charm necklace below his throat.

She'd expected there to be some kind of speech and a whole process of pomp and circumstance much like the lecture Carmichael had given her before she'd opted for imprisonment instead. That speech never came. There was no bowing, no complicated gestures, and no grand hurrah and cheers for the Black Heron's victory, only complete silence.

The leader leaned forward over the altar's edge and grasped a large, heavy metal box that hadn't been there the last time she'd seen it. He slid this toward him. When he unlatched the lid, the mechanism keeping the box intact disengaged with a series of clicks. The sides of the box fell to the table with a loud smack to reveal a two-foot-tall black obelisk of onyx, reflecting the overhead lights as perfectly as the stone bowl beside it.

The hair on the back of Lily's neck prickled and stood on end. *That's where he keeps all the stolen magic.*

Carmichael picked up the only clear vials on the table and handed one each to her and her mom. Greta bowed her head in thanks, every inch the regal Black Heron queen she pretended to be. Lily took hers gingerly with both hands and nodded briefly before she stared at the slightly cloudy potion through the glass. She held it even tighter when Carmichael put his hands on both their backs, but when Greta uncorked the vial and lifted it to her lips, she did the same.

I guess I don't have to know what it's really for as long as she does.

The minute she removed it from her mouth, the ritual chamber flared with surprising intensity. Every face and object and crevice in the stone walls clearer and brighter than if she had studied them under a microscope. Her limbs tingled with renewed energy not unlike what the Masafir's well water had given her. She sucked in a sharp breath.

A society member came to take the empty vials from them and disappeared into the crowd.

Carmichael stepped between them and spread his arms over the table. "The circle is complete."

No one said a word.

"Our time has come. Each of you, my most trusted and my greatest allies, will now enter that circle. This is our destiny and our duty. The beginning of the end before we rise to start anew."

So much for no speech. At least he kept it short.

"The Sakhan." He opened his hand, and one of the black-robed magicals around the table stepped forward to take the bone knife from the side of the obsidian bowl. This was delivered with unsurprising reverence, and when it was in the leader's hand, he turned to Greta first. "An offering from the old gods to the new."

When he held out his other hand, the woman placed

hers calmly palm-up inside his. The razor-sharp point of the knife sliced a quick incision on the pad of her thumb but she didn't make a sound. Then, he turned to Lily, and she forced herself to echo her mom's obedience.

Oddly enough, she didn't fear the edge of the blade in the man's hand. Even stranger still, she hardly felt the flesh of her thumb opening beneath the razor-sharp edge. The blood welling on her thumb, though, sparkled in the light. *It looks more like ketchup than blood. Wow, what did she put in this potion?*

"And now, we receive the gifts as they are given."

The circle of two dozen black-robed society members closed in around the table. One by one, they selected a brown glass vial from the concentric circles they'd formed and moved around the altar. They stopped at Greta first, who squeezed a drop of blood from her thumb into the vial held below it and then waited for the next.

Lily copied her mom's motions and watched her own blood swirl through the brown glass before it disappeared. She repeated the motion, standing there in a haze of black robes and shifting bodies. *I didn't think I was supposed to be able to bleed for this long.*

It caught her off guard when the shuffle of society members with vials for her to squeeze her magical blood into ended. She looked up and focused on all the faces turned toward her. As it turned out, the last vial had been for none other than Carmichael himself. The man lifted it in front of him, paused for a suspensefully long few seconds, then knocked the potion back like a shot of Jameson.

The two dozen elite of the Black Heron Society replicated the motion. Twenty-five empty vials clinked onto the stone table as one, the sound unnaturally loud. Many of the members took deep, energized breaths. A few smacked their lips and tried not to scowl at the aftertaste of iron. Most of them stared longingly at the onyx obelisk on the altar.

Carmichael tipped his head back, his eyes closed, and sucked in a hissed breath through his teeth. "Now."

Two society members standing beside each of the donors chained to the walls turned toward their victims. At the same time, the black, writhing cords of dark magic struck the prisoners in the chest—exactly like they'd struck Lily and Greta and however many other innocent people the Black Heron had taken advantage of. Most of the targets were gagged as well as chained, but that didn't stop their screams from filling the air.

With the heightened awareness brought on by her special potion, Lily couldn't have blocked out the sound even if she'd tried. She clenched her teeth as hard as she could and willed herself not to blow the whole thing and try to stop this insanity right then. *It's not the right time. Not yet. I'm so sorry.* Her jaw ached.

Waves of multi-colored magic pulsed from those chained to the wall. In an instant, each victim's magic pulsed out of them in a massive burst and streamed toward the various magical items held in clamps on the marble pillars positioned in the room. The air crackled with static and the unnerving amount of magic swelled and pulsed around them.

Carmichael turned to Lily and grinned. "It's incredible, isn't it?"

She couldn't respond and merely nodded.

The items on the pillars vibrated faster and faster. In the next moment, a black, shimmering dome of magic crackled in an arc from every clamped artifact until it connected at the ceiling in the center of the chamber and encompassed them all.

"Totems!" the leader shouted beneath the crackling dome. It sounded like thunder directly over their heads— like Lily's dream of the entire fortress caving in on itself.

Every elite magical around the altar removed something from the pockets of their robes. Stone carvings, daggers, rings, and even small jewelry boxes. One witch with yellow eyes chose a tiny ragdoll without a face as the vessel for all the magic she was about to receive.

That's what these are. They're gonna funnel all the magic into themselves through those totems.

The ground trembled beneath her with the force of all the magic present, despite the stabilizing effect of the artifacts on the marble pillars. Lily felt dizzy with energy and awareness, and she stepped forward to clutch the edge of the table to steady herself.

Greta leaned forward and pressed herself against the altar in the same way. "Lily."

She could barely hear her over the roar of the magic and the wailing of the poor people forced to power the whole thing. After a deep breath, she turned her head with a grimace.

"It's almost time. Be ready. And remember, follow my lead."

She nodded and clutched the altar even tighter. *Pay attention.*

Greta pushed herself upright from the table's edge, but not before she darted a glance at Carmichael. Lily turned a little to look at the man, whose head was still thrown back as he basked in all his plans finally brought to life. Directly in front of him, he held the stone worn smooth by so many years of the rhythmic turning in his hand.

No way. Lily bit back a gasp and quickly pushed herself upright again to stand beside Carmichael. *That's where we're gonna put it. All of it?* She wanted to turn to her mom to make sure, but the man stood directly between them and she couldn't simply step back for a private conversation in the middle of all this. She wouldn't have had the chance, anyway.

"Greta. Lily." He glanced at each of them in turn and didn't even attempt to hide the wild, feral glint in his eye. That grin was a sneer of self-important victory. "Fulfill your purpose!"

That is seriously not motivating at all. Lily continued to clench her teeth, the headache she knew she'd have later dulled by the potion running through her now.

The only thing she saw of her mom was both of Greta's arms raising from the other side of Carmichael, her hands outstretched toward the obelisk on the altar. The stone pillar filled with stolen magic and surrounded by it glistened even in the shadow of the black-magic dome surrounding them all. It looked like it was dancing, flickering with every different color and shade but always came back to the same deep, pitch-black.

I'll follow your lead. Any minute now, Mom.

A stream of the black, writhing cord burst from both Greta's palms and struck the flat, shining surface of the obelisk's side.

"What?" Lily shouted. It burst out of her mouth without warning at all. *She wants me to use the same spell they used on us? Is she crazy?*

A warm, firm hand grasped her upper arm. Carmichael leaned in close to her ear and sent a shiver of revulsion through her. She could smell his excitement—like a bowl of fruit left out in too long in the sun.

"You can do this, Lily." The man squeezed her arm even harder and gave it a shake of both reassurance and warning. "Follow your mother. Finish this."

He has no idea that's what I'm actually doing.

He released her arm with a painful jerk and nodded at the obelisk now bombarded with Greta's magic—dark magic from an Optatus witch.

With a shout of frustration, Lily raised both hands toward the Obelisk and focused. She had enough time to glance quickly at Romeo in the crowd. He stared at her with wide eyes and seemed equally as offended by what she was supposed to do as she felt. But he nodded anyway and kept his gaze trained on her.

Whatever it takes. All an Optatus witch needs is the desire to get something done. I guess I'm a dark witch for a day.

She put all her focus on the onyx obelisk on the black stone altar and let her magic do its thing.

TWENTY-FIVE

A t first, the black magic sputtered in her palms and sparked and flailed barely an inch from her hands. It was only for a second—a moment most likely unseen by everyone else, or at least overlooked. Lily pushed with her whole being and the black cord of undulating, siphoning magic burst free.

It struck the obelisk with a deafening crack, although the stone pillar itself didn't move from where it had been set.

Her focus caved in around her, all sound and sight funneled into a pinpoint of one thing and one thing only. Using this spell and making the obelisk do what she wanted.

"The Transference!" Carmichael roared.

Dozens of voices rose around her in the ritual chamber, all of them muted by the intensity of her concentration that blocked everything else out. The spell's language was one she didn't know, and her homemade magical interpreter came across its first roadblock in translating anything. She couldn't understand a word of it. *I don't want to know what they're saying. I don't need to know.*

The ground trembled beneath her. Bright flashes of light and crackling energy erupted across the black dome overhead and blazed around the stone altar like a lightning storm. The obelisk began to vibrate and the chanting grew even louder. She focused intently to hold her hand the steadiest of all of them as she maintained the spell that had been used to torture her for a week. Her mouth felt dry and even painful.

"Give it everything!" Carmichael screamed. His chanting was louder than the others as if that would add power to the magic he had no part in. This was all Lily and her mother—and it was all wrong.

The obelisk trembled where it rested on the altar and a thick, oozing trail of magic slithered from the tip of the column. Like lava pouring from the mouth of a volcano, the magic that had been stolen from hundreds of Black Heron victims spilled from the top and inched its way down the side away from the Optatus witches compelling it. Lily had no other intention with her spell but to blast away at it exactly like Greta was, but then she realized what her mom was trying to do.

Into the bowl.

A high-pitched ringing sounded from the pillar, like someone running their hand around the rim of a wineglass to make it sing. She focused her attention on driving all the contained magic into the obsidian bowl beside it on the altar. *One step at a time. Only one.*

It seemed to take forever to direct the magic to slither into the receptacle. Finally, the end of the writhing trail that glittered and swirled with so many colors left the top of the obelisk. The remainder of the magic quickly drew the last parts of it into the bowl, which released a blinding white flash. Lily blinked against the glare. The magic in the bowl sat there like a gigantic egg, contained and open for everyone to see—and to take.

Greta broke off her dark spell, stumbled forward, and thumped her hands on the altar to keep from falling.

"Mom." Lily stopped her spell too and didn't care about the ceremony rules. She stepped toward her mom and ignored Carmichael's snarl of surprise when her hip bumped against his leg. "Hey, are you okay?"

"Greta!" Carmichael barked.

"I'm fine." The woman met her daughter's gaze, her eyes burning fiercely, and spoke so quickly and so quietly that she had to try reading her lips too. "Take it back before its finished. Put it in his totem. The minute it disappears, you grab me, and you hold on tight."

"You need to get up, witch," the man ordered, although he didn't move to separate mother and daughter yet.

Lily turned to glare at him. "She needs a minute—"

"She's had all the time she needs! I swear, Greta, if you don't stand and finish this, my hand will be the last thing you ever see."

"It's only a—"

"Stop." Greta grabbed her daughter's hand and squeezed it. Then, she let go, nodded, and pushed herself up from the edge of the table. "I'm fine. Carmichael, I'm fine. I didn't eat as much as I should have."

"Finish this. Now." The man glared at his most prized witch, one hand balled into a fist at his side and the other turning the stone over and over in one smooth, repetitive motion. His totem.

"I will. Of course I will." She nodded at Lily. "Together, sweets. We're almost finished."

"Okay." She took her place beside her mom—except for Carmichael standing rigidly between them. *Don't look at the rock. Not until I have to.*

Moving as one, mother and daughter extended their hands again and released the dark rope of crackling magic meant to take it from others. The minute their spells struck the egg-shaped magic in the obsidian bowl, the swirling orb ballooned to twice its size before it shrank again. Lily focused on moving the magic out once more, and the Black Heron's chanting continued. It was faster now and more urgent, with more longing to finally reach the end of this whole ritual.

Too slowly for the young witch's liking, the magic gathered in the bowl slithered out again. Twenty-five writhing tendrils of it wiggled toward the twenty-five society members chanting over the totems clenched tightly in their hands. She almost flinched when the closest tendril skirted past her and writhed in front of her for a second before it moved aside and sniffing at Carmichael's smooth rock.

The chanting intensified, and every tendril of stolen magic struck every offered totem at the same time. A collective gasp rose from the elite around the altar as their bodies illuminated with the connection of magic to their artifacts and the totems to their bodies. Hair stood on end and robes fluttered without a breeze. The bowl vibrated on the altar.

Carmichael actually giggled.

The sound made Lily want to cringe, but she continued grimly.

The totems grew brighter and brighter as the two witches poured their power out into the bowl. Members' fingers and hands took on the same glow, which spread quickly through their bodies until their faces too, above the robes, made them all look like they stood under a bright, shining sun.

Any minute now. Lily knew she was grimacing, but she couldn't help it. There were too many other things to focus on. *It's almost gone.*

The magic in the obsidian bowl had in fact diminished significantly. It reminded her of sucking up a bead of water through one of those tiny coffee straws.

Focus.

When the magic in the bowl had dwindled to what might be equated to a few drops of water, Greta uttered a growl of intense concentration and effort.

"The mirror!" Lily screamed. It could have passed as the ramblings of a witch high on painkiller potions, out of her right mind with the effort it took her to maintain this spell most of the Black Heron Society's members could only hold for a fraction of the time.

It wasn't.

Romeo knew that too. He slapped his breastbone and

the mirror charm beneath it, his eyes clenched shut against the chaos around him. *Unravel the most powerful setback. Come on.* His palm burned over the necklace until it seared his flesh and he finally pulled away. The two dozen Black Heron elite around the altar gasped again, and he opened his eyes.

The grotesque tendrils of magic that had connected to the members' totems and were drawn into their bodies were now being drawn back out again.

"What?" a witch in front of him shouted. "This isn't right."

"What is this?"

"You assured us this would work!"

Carmichael snarled at the magic leaving the stone in his hand. "Again!"

Lily and Greta still poured the dark magic spell and two thick black columns streamed toward the bowl. But the magic had other plans, and so did they.

The chanting rose again, but it was less certain. The leader stopped to lean toward Greta. "What did you do?"

"Nothing!"

"Just focus."

Lily held back a smirk.

The magic filtered into the bowl far more quickly than it had dispersed, and when the tendrils released from all the totems, another blinding white flash filled the ritual chamber.

The Black Heron's elite members screamed in unison.

Multi-colored streams poured from their totems into the obsidian bowl and swirled against the stolen magic already gathered there. None of them could pull their hands away or do a single thing to stop it.

The most powerful setback.

Twenty-four society members bucked and writhed around the altar, rendered completely immobile as their bodies and their magic betrayed them. Eyes rolled back and jaws clenched tight. The hands around the totems were now claws, and all their magic was sucked out of them.

Except for Carmichael's.

"Greta." He stared at her with wide eyes. "What is this?"

She turned toward him with fire in her eyes and sneered. "It's for you."

The minute she said it, Lily changed the direction of the spell, as did her mother. The magic inside the bowl—now twice its original size—burst in a single column toward Carmichael and the smooth rock in his hand.

"Ha!" The man's good eye bulged in his head and the false white orb of glass reflected the multi-colored blast of magic that filtered into his stone. His chest heaved as he stared at all the power coursing into his totem to make it glow a bright white. "Greta, you—ha!"

By the time the bodies of the twenty-four elite fell at the same time, the obsidian bowl on the altar was completely empty. With another bright burst and a crack, the rest of the doubled stolen magic surged into Carmichael's totem. The two witches severed the cord of their dark magic used for only this purpose.

Lily's chest heaved with the effort, but she didn't feel

any more exhausted than when she'd started. *Not until this potion wears off.*

Carmichael shouted in triumph and stared at the glowing, trembling rock now clenched in his hand. "It's mine. All of it!" A deep, throaty cackle burst from his mouth, and he threw his head back, completely unaware of the fact that none of the magic caught in his totem had moved into him at all.

He thrust the stone into the air and roared, "You see? You see what can be done with the power of these women standing in front of you? We will be unstoppable! We will—"

A blood-curdling scream came from the far end of the ritual chamber. He jerked his hand down to his chest to protect his precious glowing rock. All heads turned toward the short, stocky magical at the back of the chamber who sagged against the chains put there to hold him up. The minute his knees touched the floor and the rest of him only dangled there from his wrists, the black dome around the gathered society members sputtered, flashed a few times, and fizzled.

"No!" Carmichael pointed at the man. "Get it to—"

Greta lunged toward him and snatched the stone out of his hand.

"What—"

She spun and launched it toward the other end of the ritual chamber.

The rest happened almost too rapidly to follow. Carmichael screamed and leapt toward Greta. Lily took her chance and blasted him with a compulsive force that catapulted him into the crowd of his followers huddled so close together behind him.

When her mother clapped her hands together, it echoed in the chamber ten times louder than it should have. She whipped her arms apart, and the black cloud of her Optatus magic erupted from her to follow the glowing rock that rocketed through the air. The black cloud swarmed around the stone before it hit the far edge of the altar. In the next moment, her magic and Carmichael's stone vanished.

Lily unleashed her Optatus magic a second later and a roiling black cloud bloomed from her palms and her chest. The cloud surged through the ritual chamber, growing and rumbling, and sparked with bright white light as it blocked everything else quickly from view. "Romeo!"

The society members shouted and screamed and scrambled over each other to see. Attack spells hurtled in all directions to strike everything but their intended targets. Then, she saw him surge through her spell and scramble to reach her. She clutched his hand as Greta wrapped a painfully strong grasp around her wrist. The chamber filled completely with black smoke, and the last thing she saw was Carmichael's snarling face and wild eyes as he dove toward her mother.

TWENTY-SIX

The ground came up to meet her at incredible speed. Lily grunted, the wind knocked completely out of her, and rolled down the side of whatever hill they'd landed on.

"Lily!" Romeo shouted.

She pushed herself up, shook her head, and didn't have time to think about the weird color of the grass beneath her hands.

"I'll kill you for this!" Carmichael roared and flung spell after spell in impressively quick succession—blue flames, a lashing purple jolt of energy, and pointed darts of red light that exploded on impact. Every time, Greta deflected his attacks with ease when she raised warded shields and heavy nets of power that absorbed everything the man sent her way.

He stumbled toward her, unrelenting in his pointless attack until finally, she flicked her hand toward him. Her magic knocked his feet out from under him and thrust him forward. He met the grass face-first but scrambled to one knee with a snarl and stopped.

Greta twirled a ball of black, swirling magic in her hand in exactly the same way he had twirled his all-important totem until she'd snatched it away.

Breathing heavily, he wiped the foamy spit from his lips and goatee. "Where did you send it?"

"By the time you find it, it'll already be somewhere else." Her calm, impassive expression embodied everything Lily knew about her mom. "I think you lost your chance, Carmichael. You let it slip right through your fingers."

With a growl of rage, the man lurched to his feet and barreled toward her again.

She clapped her hands together and drew them apart enough to threaten him with more of what she and her daughter had unleashed in his stronghold. The man skidded to a halt on the grass, his arms flailing. "Be very, very sure of what you decide to do next."

For the first time, real fear showed in the man's eye. The false one even seemed a little dimmer, but maybe that was simply the lighting there. Wherever that was.

"Optatus." He spat it out like a curse.

Greta shrugged, and her smile widened.

"I took it from you."

"You know, that was so long ago, I hardly remember." She forced her hands together without so much as blinking. Whether it was real or not, she curled one fist inside her other palm and held it out toward him as a warning. All she had to do was open her hand, and she would end him. "You can't take the stars out of the sky, Carmichael.

But a few clouds will make it look like they were never there."

The man shifted uncomfortably and his face wavered between rage, desperation, and something Lily thought looked like regret. Then, he glanced at her where she'd rolled a few feet down the hill. "And what will you do with her?"

"She's my daughter. What do you think?"

Carmichael snarled again, but he didn't move to attack. This time, he fumbled in his back pocket and retrieved a round, flat disk. He shook it at Greta, then curled it in his own fist and glared at her. "I will find you."

She grinned. "You always do."

"And we'll finish what you started."

"If that's what you really want. Sure."

With a final glance at Lily, Carmichael opened his fist and slapped his other hand against the silver disk. In an instant, he was gone.

That spurred Lily and Romeo into action. He ran toward her, sliding down the hillside, and she began to scramble toward her mother.

"Lily, are you okay?" He reached her and wrapped his arms around her.

She let herself relax in his embrace for a few seconds, taking in the earthy smell of him tinged with something like oranges now. A different smell but still him.

When he pulled her away by the shoulders and examined her, his eyes were wide with concern. "Will you at least say something?"

A hoarse puff of laughter escaped her, and she cupped his face. "I'm fine. All good."

"Yeah?" He nodded vigorously, still lost and unable to believe what he saw in front of him. "I have no idea what happened in there, but I...you..."

"You did great." She slid her hand to the back of his neck and held him there, mainly to get him to stop nodding. "Really. It was perfect."

"Yeah?"

"Yeah."

"Okay..."

She laughed and held his gaze. "Are you okay?"

"I still don't know." An uncertain smile lifted the corners of his mouth. "I can't believe that actually happened."

"Well, it did." Greta moved slowly down the hill toward them and her feet brushed almost soundlessly over the soft grass. "You were both wonderful."

Lily didn't look away from Romeo for a few seconds but finally pulled herself together enough to release him and step back. "We did it."

"You did it, sweets." Her mother's brows drew together in sympathy. "I merely laid out the path. I'm so sorry you had to walk it the way you did."

Swallowing the lump in her throat, Lily stepped toward her mom. *If she hugs me like she did in that stupid reliquary, there's gonna be an Optatus witch-off. And I'll win.* She stopped in front of her and saw no hint of the dazed glassiness in her mom's eyes or the vacant lack of emotion. "Do you feel like yourself again?"

Greta chuckled. "Do you?"

Lily couldn't hold back any longer, and she rushed to hug the woman as tightly as she possibly could. Her nose burned, warning her of the tears she wouldn't let fall. Not right now. "I'm sorry it took me so long."

The woman ran her hands over her daughter's hair, then stopped to pull out one of the shimmering black gems studded through her braids. She rested her cheek on the top of her head and sighed. "I knew you'd find me and never doubted that. You know, the funny thing is I don't know how long it actually did take."

Romeo cleared his throat. "About three months. Give or take."

Lily pulled slowly away from her mother's embrace to search for a reaction.

Greta merely nodded slowly and tilted her head. "Huh. That's it?"

"They were a very long three months," she said. "But I know sitting in a stone box will warp your sense of time."

Her mom chuckled. "Well, yeah. There is that. I only... You realize it took me seven years to set this up, right? And you only needed three months."

She glanced at Romeo, who simply shrugged and continued to look at Greta. "You made it fairly easy."

The woman released her daughter's shoulders with wide eyes and stepped back. "No, I didn't. The only reason it was easy for you is because you're you."

"Optatus." Lily took a deep breath. "Like you."

"Exactly like me, sweets. It's in your blood and everything."

"Yeah, so I've heard." She glanced at the cut on her thumb from the bone knife, which had stopped bleeding some time during their serious spellcasting. "While we're on the subject of what and who we are, Mom, what was that?"

"What was what?"

"That." She gestured toward the top of the hill. "With Carmichael. He's not merely some guy who abducted you, tortured you, and tried to brainwash you into turning all magic upside down, is he?"

Greta closed her eyes and exhaled a long sigh. "We have a lot to talk about."

"Yeah, we do. Which is why I'm asking right now."

Nodding, her mom squinted up at the sky and shrugged. "I'll tell you everything, Lily. I will. Right now, we need to find shelter and a safer place to rest. Then we can swap battle stories, huh?"

"I won't wait any more simply to get a few—Mom. Mom!"

Her mother didn't turn as she stalked away over the rolling hills, hiking the ridiculous green gown up enough to quicken her stride. "I think it's gonna rain."

Lily groaned and looked at the sky. There weren't any clouds, but now that she had a brief moment of absolutely nothing to do and no plans to fulfill, she could really see the sky and wondered why it was completely pink—every-where and with no sun.

Romeo climbed the rest of the hill until he stood beside her and spun in a full, slow circle. "Okay, maybe it's only me. I know being a werewolf with new magic from witches is kinda uncharted territory for…everyone. Mostly. But does this grass look purple to you?"

As she looked down again to watch her mom walking away from her, Lily nodded. "Yep. Pink sky. Purple grass. Lady in a green dress headed off again and doing whatever she wants."

He nudged her arm and leaned toward her. "You know you're wearing a green dress too, right?"

"Yeah, and I hate it." When she looked at him, they both chuckled.

"I can't believe I'm saying this, Lil. It feels weird to laugh."

"There's a week in the worst hotel ever for ya." She took his hand and nodded down the hill toward her mother. "I guess we're gonna keep chasing my mom for a while."

"Well, at least we can see her this time."

"Not for long if we don't hurry up."

TWENTY-SEVEN

Lily and Romeo followed Greta Antony across the rolling hills of purple grass. In only a few minutes, they stood in front of a forest that hadn't been there until it simply appeared.

The older woman stopped at the edge of the trees—blue bark and blue branches with purple leaves and bright, shimmering gold flowers—and gestured for them to hurry up. "I wasn't kidding about the rain."

"What rain—"

A thunderous crack rent the air directly above them, and Lily flinched. The purple grass dotting the hillsides pulsed with a light violet glow and every individual strand stood straight up and quivered rigidly.

"Ow." She picked her feet up and tried to tiptoe over the blades of grass that were now almost literal blades. They didn't budge at all under her weight. "What is this?"

"Okay." Romeo scooped her up and carried her the rest of the way toward the trees.

With a short laugh, she wound her arms around his neck and grinned at him. "So they even gave you shoes, huh?"

"Yep. The whole shebang. Reserved only for special hybrids."

"Look at you two." Greta leaned back against a blue tree trunk, her arms folded as she smiled at them. "I gotta tell ya, this is exactly how I imagined you guys together when you grew up."

"You imagined us together?" Lily grimaced as he stepped through the tree line and slid her hand down his neck as he set her gently on the soft forest floor. Apparently, the moss grew in shades of purple too, but at least it wouldn't cut her feet.

"Of course. You two were glued together at the hip."

The werewolf wiggled his eyebrows and bumped his hip against Lily's. She snorted and slapped his arm.

"Julian and I used to sit up after you'd fallen asleep and talk about what it would be like to see our kids all grown up and going on adventures together—and probably getting into trouble."

"And you imagined it like this?" She gestured to the stupid green dress.

Her mother grimaced and shook her head. "Not exactly. I honestly wasn't sure who you'd turn to for help with this, sweets. But you made the perfect choice."

Romeo grinned. "I'll take that as a compliment."

"It was." Pushing herself off the tree, Greta studied the young werewolf—hybrid, now, if they were splitting hairs—

and took a deep breath. "You look so much like your dad, Romeo. Only taller."

He laughed. "And better looking, I hope."

She tilted her head from one side to the other with a noncommittal hum. Then, she pulled him into a hug. His eyes flew wide in surprise but he wrapped his arms slowly around her while he stared at Lily. This time, she shrugged in response and simply watched them.

This is weird. I thought we'd pick up right where we left off, but...something's wrong.

With a sigh and a curt nod, Greta pulled away from the man she'd known as a boy and studied him again. "How is your dad, by the way?"

"Oh. Uh...he's good. I think. He's probably waiting for another phone call, actually. But he's good."

She nodded again with a tiny frown, then patted his shoulders and released him. "Good. I'm glad. Let's, uh... step a little bit farther into the trees, huh?"

"Mom."

The minute Greta gestured toward the open purple hills beyond the forest, another crack of thunder made the ground shudder beneath them. Huge, flaming yellow drops of something that couldn't possibly be rain poured in a sudden sheet from the pink sky. The purple grass sizzled and smoked when the fiery rain fell but not a single blade moved. They merely pulsed with a brighter light.

"I know where we are and I know we don't belong here. We can stay for a little while, but as soon as we can leave, we should." The woman lowered her hand and nodded toward the thickening forest behind her. "Okay?"

"Yep."

"No problem."

The young couple tore themselves away from the sight of the burning rain and the knifelike grass and followed her through the trees.

"It's not gonna rain in here, is it?" he asked and ducked instinctively as he looked at the thick branches and even thicker purple foliage overhead.

"Definitely not. The trees get something else entirely. But that grass out there can get a little...aggressive."

"Really." Lily shot her friend a look, and he stifled a chuckle. "Where are we going?"

"It should be a little bit farther up here." Greta pointed through the trees at absolutely nothing but more trees. "Then we can sit and finally have that chat. I owe you that much."

"Yep," her daughter muttered. "So we'll go a little farther. But where is here, exactly."

"When we get there, Lily."

"Mom, do you even know where you're going?"

Greta stopped short, turned quickly, and frowned. "Of course I know where I'm going. Granted, I've never actually been here before, but I know this place like the back of my—"

"What?" Lily leaned forward a little, hoping she'd heard something very different than what her mom had actually said. "You've never been here."

"That's what I said." The woman's gaze moved quickly through the trees, scanned the ground, then moved up toward the canopy before it settled on her daughter. "You of all people should know that simply because you haven't physically been somewhere doesn't mean you haven't seen it. Or that you don't know what you'll find when you get there."

She opened her mouth to spout something angry and defensive, but all that came out was a puff of air. "Yeah, okay. I have nothing."

"So you've only seen this place in visions," Romeo said as they started moving again. "Like Lily's."

"Not...exactly." Greta paused, peered around a few trees, then nodded and veered to the right.

"I can't believe this." Lily dragged her hands down her face, then elbowed Romeo in the side. "Is this how you felt the entire time we followed visions and a giant beam of light that only I could see?"

He smirked and rubbed the back of his neck. "Okay, I didn't spend three months chasing you across four different continents in a Winnebago. Only seven years hoping you'd show up and ask me to do something crazy."

"What?"

The werewolf stared straight ahead. "Huh?"

She shot him a playful frown. "We can talk about that one later too, okay?"

"Yep. I only meant that it was different with us, Lil. I was there with you from beginning to end. The whole time. We met the same people and fought the same battles. Until the whole 'cage 'em and torture 'em separately' thing." He laughed a little, then cut it short and frowned at the fact that he'd actually said that. "But it's different with your mom. You guys haven't done all this stuff together."

"Right." She watched her mother pick her way through the trees. *She's moving like she's on her own again. But she's probably listening to everything we say, too.* "We've been on many trips together, sure. But I don't know this side of her."

"You know." Romeo nodded and slipped his hand into hers. "You simply haven't seen it before."

"That's exactly what she said to try to convince me that we're not simply walking aimlessly through a purple forest."

"Purple-ish blue, really." He jerked his head toward her and grinned.

"Yeah, okay."

"Here." Greta stopped, turned toward them, and pointed ahead and a little to the right. "It's right here. Exactly like I knew it would be."

When the woman strode off through the trees again without waiting for them, Lily shook her head. "It's like chasing a kid through the mall."

Romeo chuckled.

They soon reached the tree where Greta had stopped and turned to look at whatever amazing thing she'd found. Lily's mouth dropped open. "Okay... I'll give it to her on this one."

"Maybe we should've been more excited."

"I don't know if that would've made a difference."

He shrugged. "You're probably right."

Greta had led them to a clearing in the blue-treed forest, where soft purple moss and clover covered the ground in an almost perfect circle. The trees surrounding their clearing stretched their closest branches all the way overhead to form a tented canopy of leaves and kept the fiery rain successfully at bay. In the center of the clearing was an iron brazier about five feet tall, already stacked with dry purple wood and ringed by a circle of glowing white stones. Purple tree stumps surrounded the brazier, and behind the pseudo firepit were two neon-green tents—the kind with four straight walls, an entrance flap that went all the way to the ceiling, and enough room to set up a king-sized bed and all kinds of other items on the inside.

Lily cleared her throat. "So..."

Greta was already seated on one of the tree stumps around the brazier and she spread her arms and grinned. "Welcome to Kahara."

Romeo leaned toward Lily and muttered, "Have you ever heard of this place?"

"Nope."

"Great. The surprises keep coming."

She squeezed his hand and walked forward with him into the clearing.

TWENTY-EIGHT

"Wow, you weren't kidding." Romeo stared at the massive woven pale-purple basket in Greta's arms. The entrance flap to the tent on the right fell back into place behind her, and she hoisted the basket toward him and Lily where they sat on purple tree stumps around the brazier.

"It's always set up and ready to go." The woman placed the basket on the ground between Lily and the tree stump she chose for herself, then dusted her hands off with a little sigh. "I've heard there's something particularly special about the food here."

"You mean besides the fact that it looks like an Andy Warhol painting in 3D?" The young witch raised an eyebrow at the neon-colored fruits, most of which resembled varieties she recognized. She couldn't even begin to name some of them, though.

"Yes, Lily. Besides that." Greta reached into the basket and pulled out what looked like a blueberry—except for the fact that it was the size of an apple and an even brighter neon-pink than the sky. "Here's to finding truth in the legends, huh?"

She stared as her mom bit into her choice and waited for a reaction. Although she wasn't sure what she expected, it wasn't eye-roll and the deep sigh of satisfaction as bright pink juice dribbled down her chin.

"It tastes like banana bread."

"Weird."

"Do you wanna try?" She held the fruit toward her daughter, but Lily shook her head.

"How 'bout one of these purple...apples?" Romeo stood to stretch past Lily into the basket. When he sat and bit into the fruit, he hummed in surprise and kept chewing. "It definitely tastes like an apple. Or apple cider."

She laughed. "Those are basically the same thing."

"No, I mean the kind in the bottles we used to pop for New Year's." He took another huge bite and crunched happily. "With bubbles."

"Huh."

"Lily, you really should eat something." Her mother finished the last of the giant fruit and wiped the juice from her chin with the back of her hand. "It'll make you feel better."

The young witch sighed and clasped her hands together. "Okay, look. We're in a place where all the colors are wrong and it rains fire on literal blades of grass. Before that, we performed the most insane ritual magic inside the High Seat of the most insane magicals from all over the world. And somewhere in between, you had a secret, coded conversation with the man who imprisoned both of us. I'm not hungry."

"Come on, sweets—"

"Mom. I want to know what's going on."

"And you will." Greta scrabbled in the basket to withdraw a bunch of orange grapes on a blue vine, except each individual grape was shaped like a banana. "Ooh, these look good."

I can't keep looking at those and take myself seriously at the same time. "I know you're stalling."

The woman paused with a banana-grape halfway to her mouth, glanced at Romeo, then slowly lowered all the fruit into her lap.

Lily shook her head. "And now that only makes me want to hear what you have to tell us even more—and even sooner."

She extended the vine of weird grapes toward her, but her daughter pushed them away. "Okay, fine. If I start talking now—which is, admittedly, sooner than I wanted to —will you at least start eating."

"I'll give you a five-minute head start."

Greta blinked. "That's really nothing in the scheme of things, is it? Deal."

Lily straightened on the tree stump. She wanted to cross her legs but was unable to do so in the stupid green dress. Impatient, she widened her eyes and gestured for her mom to continue.

Popping the first mini-banana in her mouth, Greta released a small laugh. "Seriously, you have to try one of these. They are chocolate-flavored."

"Mom!"

"Okay, okay." Her mother flinched jokingly, hunched her shoulders, and nodded as she set the bunch of weird fruit in the basket. Romeo stood again to quickly swipe a handful of the same from the vine before he sat again. The woman smirked at him, then clasped her hands together and exhaled a quick, heavy breath. "This circle around this fire was made for spinning truths. For starting one thread and winding it all the way back until the beginning becomes the end."

"I'm not new to the concept of telling stories around a campfire." Lily cocked her head. "All three of us have done that before. Together."

"Right." Greta cleared her throat. "You sure are putting me in a tight spot, sweets."

"No, I'm not."

Her mom pursed her lips and tried to hide a smile. "Let me set the scene, okay?"

With a flick of her wrists, she pushed the long sleeves of her gown up and snorted. "I'd burn this thing right now if they left us any clothes."

"Who's that?" Romeo had moved on to other freaky flora from this weird place they had never heard of.

"Whoever was here before us." Greta winked at him and flicked her fingers at the brazier. A blaze of green and indigo flames shot up around the blue wood chopped and arranged carefully in the center of the huge metal dish. "Now, I can start."

"Please do." Lily stared at the fire, which moved like

any other fire but had some alien quality she couldn't quite put her finger on. It was also vaguely familiar.

"Let me start with where we are. Right here, in this circle, and then on a broader scale."

"Kahara." The green fire danced in Lily's eyes. "That's where you said we were."

"That's the clearing, yes. A kind of pit-stop for the weary traveler but always a last resort."

"Why?" Romeo slurped the brown juice dripping from his mouth and tried to wipe it all away. Lily snorted when she saw him fumble with his own mess and shook her head.

Her mother looked at him with a small frown. "Because you can only ever open the door once."

"You mean if we leave and get lost in this totally weird forest, we won't be able to come back?" She frowned at her mom and watched the light and shadows from the fire flicker across Greta's face.

"No, Kahara is here as long as we are. I'm talking about Mabayn. The entire world around us." Greta glanced at the basket of fruit, decided against making another selection, and folded her hands in her lap. "So this is my first and last time here. I'm merely trying to make the most of it."

"What about us?"

"You, my warrior daughter, can come back to Mabayn as many times as there are people in your path who can and will bring you here again. The first time you open the door yourself will be your last visit. So keep that in mind before you knock."

"Mom, I don't even know what this is, let alone how to get here."

"Good." Greta nodded. "It took me years to understand it, and I hope you spend your time doing something much more productive."

No one said anything else for a few more seconds. Lily wanted to grab her mom and shake her by the shoulders and force her to continue the explanations she was so obviously reluctant to start in the first place. Then she caught her mom glancing pointedly at the basket of fruit on the ground between them. "Oh, jeez. Fine."

The minute she snatched up a marbled fruit like an orange but with bright-blue kiwi fuzz, Greta turned her attention back to the fire. *Kiwi fuzz, or the blue in blue cheese. This is ridiculous.* She dug her finger into the outer layer like an orange and began to peel it. The scent of key lime pie filled the air.

"So." The woman nodded at the green and indigo flames. "Mabayn doesn't technically exist."

Lily almost dropped the orange-kiwi-cheeseball, and Romeo choked on whatever he was stuffing into his face.

"Not that we don't exist. We obviously do." Greta smoothed the few stray strands of hair that had broken free of her braids away from her forehead, then stopped to pick out one of the stones. The fire spat and released a puff of bright-pink smoke into the sky when she flicked the stone into the brazier. "I guess you could think of this whole place as a different plane. Maybe even a different dimension."

She glanced at the young couple, who both stared at her with wide eyes.

Lily finally managed to speak. "You teleported us to a different dimension."

"Sure."

"Hey." Romeo shrugged and wiped his hands on his pants. "If it got us out of that place and to where those people can't follow us, I'm all for it."

"If any of those people knew how to access Mabayn, I'll strip down naked and dance around this fire."

"Mom."

The werewolf swallowed. "If I say anything right now, it's gonna sound so messed up."

Greta chuckled. "This plane belongs to magic entirely. The storytellers use it and a few other wandering tribes."

"Like the Masafir." Lily leaned forward and rested her forearms on her thighs.

"Yeah." Her mom shot her a playful frown. "Where'd you hear about those?"

"I didn't." Grinning, she raised her eyebrows. "We met them."

"Seriously?"

"And I didn't like any of it." Romeo shook his head slowly and eyed the basket of food but didn't move to take anything else. "Those people were... I mean, I don't even know if they were people."

"They're people as much as that fruit is fruit." Greta nodded at the basket.

"So kind of and kind of not." Lily nodded and absently put a section of the weird orange-shaped something in her mouth. *Yep. Definitely key lime pie.* "Do you know anything else about them?"

"Only that they tend to spend ninety-nine-point-nine percent of their time unseen and unheard by most people everywhere." Her mother laughed. "And you met them."

"Oh, yeah." She sat up and waved a hand like it was nothing. "They brought us into their secret oasis in the desert, gave us water, stuck us in a room full of mirrors for a couple of prophecies. No big deal."

"You, my love, will have to sit down with me one day very soon and tell me every single detail of that encounter." Her mom shook her head in amazement. "The Masafir are something I haven't yet seen."

Lily grinned. "Sure." *So why does she suddenly look so sad?*

"Anyway." Greta slapped her thighs. "We came here because it was the first thing that popped into my head when the shield around Carmichael's altar conveniently gave out at the perfect moment. I honestly thought there would be more fighting."

"Wait, what?" She frowned and glanced around the clearing. "I thought that was part of your plan."

The woman snorted and flicked another one of the black stones from her hair into the fire. "Definitely not. Okay, I hoped something like that would come along when the time was right. Things usually work out far better that way. We wouldn't have been able to go anywhere with that shield up and especially powered by ten stabilizing artifacts. But you, my brilliantly scheming offspring, would have come up with something on the spot if you had to. I'm sure of it."

"Probably." Lily shrugged, definitely aware of the warm thrill of pride spreading through her chest. But it was short-lived. "Where did you send that stone pumped full of everyone's magic, by the way?"

"Well... I'm not exactly sure."

Romeo coughed and waved dismissively when Lily turned to look at him.

She opened her mouth, closed it, and took a short breath. "Say that again."

"By not exactly, I mean not exactly. The intention behind teleporting something that powerful was simply to send it somewhere safe. Where someone we could trust would find it and keep it safe until we decided what to do with it."

"So it's with someone you know, then." She rubbed her lips a few times but knew it didn't make her look any less skeptical.

"Probably. Maybe." Greta pointed at her. "You added as much of your magic to the spell as I did. So theoretically, it could be with someone you know."

Lily bit down on her tongue and tried to smile. "Huh."

"We know many people, guys," Romeo muttered.

"If we narrow it down to the people we trust factor, it really shouldn't be that hard to find." Greta raised her arms in a careful stretch and scowled at the way the ridiculous green gown constricted the movement. "I wouldn't worry about it."

"So coming here wasn't part of your plan, either," Lily said.

"Nope. And here we are."

"And how do we get out?"

Greta licked her lips, smacked them a few times, and stared at the emerald flames in the brazier. "I have no idea."

TWENTY-NINE

"Oh, my God..." Lily dragged her hands down both sides of her face before bending over her thighs again and hanging her head. "You're kidding."

"If I was, I'm fairly sure you wouldn't find my jokes very funny anyway."

For a few seconds, she couldn't think of anything to say. *Even Greta Antony doesn't know how to get us out of this one.* She felt her mom's gaze on her all the same and managed to come up with, "You have your moments."

"And this is definitely not one of them. I know, sweets. I'm sorry."

"Okay, or we could look at it this way." Romeo spread his arms and glanced at the clearing around them. "A prison in another dimension ruled by magic is a million times better than a stone prison ruled by a complete lunatic."

Both witches turned to look at him in silence. Lily squinted.

"It's only a thought, okay? I'm trying to lighten the suddenly despairing mood you two are whippin' up over there." He shrugged. "Carry on."

"You're right, though." Greta nodded. "This place is far better than where we were. And definitely safer."

Lily ran the sole of her foot across the soft purple moss. "Okay. So that means we have more than enough time to put our heads together and find a way to get back to...what? The real world?"

"This world is equally as real, Lily." Greta rolled her shoulders and rocked her head from side to side. A series of pops worked their way up her spine. "And I said safer. Not completely safe. Mabayn comes with its own set of dangers."

"Awesome." Romeo flicked his hand toward the ground and a yellow bolt of light surged from his fingertip and singed a surprisingly large hole in the clover beside his foot. "Oh, come on!"

"Are you okay over there, werewitch?" Greta raised an eyebrow and stared at the hole in the ground.

"I did not mean to do that. Promise." He pulled his gaze away from his unintended destruction and scowled at the woman. "And can we please come up with something other than werewitch? I'm not a fan."

"Whatever you decide, bud, I'm behind it a hundred percent." She gave him a thumbs-up.

"Oh, man." Lily rubbed her temple and tried to forget that the last minute had ever happened. "Seriously, Mom, what kind of danger are you talking about?"

"The kind that I'll probably be able to explain more when we find it. Or when it finds us."

"That means you don't know."

Greta snorted and stared at her daughter. "Do you want me to start listing at least a hundred things, or would you like to spend the time we have not running and fighting to get us all on the same page so we can go home?"

Yep. Now we're picking up right where we left off six months ago. The thought made her smirk and it broadened into a grin. "You've always been good at multitasking."

Her mom tried to keep a straight face, but the fact that they'd fallen back into their usual battle-of-the-wills arguments now of all times made them both laugh. "I really taught you well, didn't I?"

Lily shrugged. "If you say so."

"But not nearly well enough." Greta stuck her bare foot out to brush it playfully against her daughter's leg. "That's a compliment, sweets. You did so much more in less time than I could have ever managed. And what you learned along the way is beyond anything I could have possibly shown you."

She sighed. "But you showed me how. That's what matters."

"Sorry..." Romeo scratched the back of his head and leaned toward the Antony witches. "Did you say a hundred dangers in this magical dimension?"

"Give or take. We're not gonna worry about any of that until we actually have a reason to." Greta nodded at him with a very serious frown that was supposed to be reassuring.

Romeo stood again to stretch over Lily and into the basket of neon fruit. "I'm not worried."

Lily leaned away so he could reach more easily and smirked at him.

He paused before he sat again, saw her looking at him, and gave her a quick kiss on the cheek. "I'm not."

"Good." She watched him sit and pressed her lips together to restrain her smile.

"Good." Greta echoed and rubbed her hands as if they were seated in front of the green fire on a cold night instead of in the middle of a perfectly comfortable day in Mabayn. "So we're finished with storytime, then."

"No." She pointed at her mom. "You can't get away with only half of it."

"Lily, I told you everything I know about this place, minus the danger list. Can we simply call that mostly covered and go into the various details later?"

"After you tell me about Carmichael, sure."

Greta stared at her and wrinkled her nose. "You're really not gonna let this one go, are you?"

"Mom, if I let things go that easily, I would've never made it halfway across the world to find you."

"Touché." Sucking a leftover fruit piece out of her teeth, Greta returned her attention to the fire and stared at it for a few moments, unmoving. "His full name is Oliver Bastion Cantus."

Romeo snorted. "And he opted for Carmichael?"

"I guess. I never heard anyone call him that until his fun-loving friends shoved me through the front doors of the High Seat. Honestly, I prefer Oliver."

"Because you like the way it sounds, or..." She gestured for her mom to keep going.

"You have to understand, Lily. There are so many things I haven't told you because by the time I could have, it simply didn't matter anymore. And by the time it mattered, I couldn't tell you." A wry chuckle escaped her. "I promise it's not any kind of secret I'm trying to keep from you."

"You sure are working it up to sound like a secret you're trying to keep from me." The young witch picked another piece of the odd fruit loose and stuck more fibrous key lime pie in her mouth.

"I'm not. It's merely complicated."

"That's never the right answer for anything." Romeo's wide eyes moved from Greta and onto the fire. "Trust me."

"So uncomplicate it," Lily added.

"I've known Oliver since we were kids, okay? He was... Honestly, he was my version of your Romeo."

"Your what?"

The werewolf chuckled and rocked a little on the tree stump. "Your Romeo. I could get used to that."

"Mom, are you insane?"

"For having friends? Please, Lily. You're too smart for that."

She leaned away from her mother and her face felt like it couldn't decide what expression to make. "No, I mean... Romeo and I are..." *What? We're together, right? And I can't simply say it in the same conversation as thinking about my mom with—* She cleared her throat and had to shake the image from her head.

"What, you think that he and I..." Greta rolled her eyes. "That's not what I mean. He was my best friend for a long time, Lily. We grew up together. Oliver was the only person in my life who was there for me through everything. He was the only person I could talk to and we were connected at the hip. Most of the time, it was like we could read each other's minds. Don't tell me you have no idea what I'm talking about."

"This isn't about me."

"That's exactly what we are, Lil."

She turned and shot Romeo a warning glance. "It's not about you, either. Or what we are."

"It's not like I could see the future and know what he'd end up doing almost twenty-five years later." Greta scoffed.

Lily froze. "Twenty-five or almost twenty-five?"

"What?

"Years, Mom."

"Almost. That's what I said."

Her daughter hunched her shoulders—which seemed the only appropriate response when she couldn't simply bound up from the tree trunk and storm through the forest with a whole unexplained danger list—and forced them down again. "How many years?"

"Twenty-three. And a half. Maybe." Her mom's lips were pressed together in a rigid line, all other expression removed from her face completely.

Her angry face and her guilty face are exactly the same things. And now, I can't not ask the question she already knows I'm gonna ask. Lily exhaled a long, forceful breath. "Is that man my dad?"

"What? No, Lily, he's not your dad."

"Mom..."

"Your father is...who knows where, if he's even alive. And I really don't care. But I swear on your grandfather's ashes that it's not Oliver."

"Stop calling him that."

"Why?"

"Because it makes it feel like this whole thing was a personal vendetta you dragged me into simply to make a point!" When she stopped shouting, she realized that she'd leapt to her feet and now towered over her mother with her fists clenched at her sides.

The huge, partially eaten fruit in Romeo's hand fell on the purple clover with a muted thud.

Greta's jaw worked in restrained anger, but her words carried the calm, collected tone Lily hated. "Sit down."

Trembling, she forced herself to comply, not because she wanted to obey the command but because she wanted to hear exactly what the woman came up with this time. "Okay. How are you gonna talk your way out of this one?"

"With the truth, Lily. That's all I've ever given you."

"Wrapped in puzzles and riddles and visions—super illuminating."

"The truth can take more shapes than you can possibly imagine, sweets," Greta said softly. "That doesn't make it any less true."

In the few strained seconds of silence, Romeo leaned forward on the tree stump to retrieve his dropped snack and dusted off the specks of blue dirt coating the bite marks.

"So what happened?"

"He wanted something I couldn't give him. That was right after I found out I was pregnant with you—my kid. And I couldn't..." Greta bit her lip and shook her head. "That ended our friendship and any opportunity for him to keep pushing. I only saw him once more after that, maybe a month later. We both knew what I was back then —that I had Optatus magic running through my veins like you. I was his first test subject with the spell that takes the magic from others. And Oli—Carmichael thought he'd stolen what made me an Optatus witch simply out of anger and because he could. I let him believe what he wanted to believe because it meant I never had to see him again."

"But you did."

"Lily, I promise you I didn't see him again until his men dragged me inside that castle...thing."

Breathing heavily through her nose, Lily nodded. "Did you start this whole wild goose chase around the Black Heron only to get to him?"

"Of course not. I knew as much about the person at the top of that pyramid as you did when you finally got there. Trust me. It was one of the biggest surprises of my life and not the good kind."

"Okay." She studied her mother's eyes—their intensity and the green flames reflected in the light-blue. "Okay. I believe you."

Greta huffed out a relieved laugh. "Good. Because I wouldn't have been able to come up with anything else to say."

"It took you long enough to say as much as you did."

Lily let herself smile a little. *At least she didn't give me the worst possible answer.*

A long, low bellow carried through the trees like a hunting horn amplified through the largest sound system in the world. All three of them looked up and searched for the sound that came from behind the tents. It sent a shiver crawling up Lily's spine.

"Do you have any idea what that could be?" Romeo cast Greta a pointed glance and nodded toward the forest.

"A few." She frowned. "But it's too far away to be a threat to us right now. And I think we could all use a little rest and more silence."

When her mom stood from the tree stump, she suddenly looked as tired as Lily had expected her to look when she'd first stepped into Carmichael's reliquary. "Rest."

"Yes, Lily." Greta rubbed her forehead. "There's a large, incredibly comfortable-looking bed in that tent, and I assume the other one is very much the same, if not exactly identical. So...wake me if you hear anything closer than a few hundred feet."

"Greta, that's really close." Romeo chucked the core of the fruit he'd finished across the clearing and into the trees.

"Well, you have a werewolf's keen sense of hearing and now, you have a little extra magic to go with it." She gave him a pert smile and stooped to kiss Lily on the forehead. When she pulled away, she cupped her daughter's cheek and studied her bright blue eyes for a few seconds. "Only you, sweets...you're incredible."

Greta lowered her hand with a tired smile, stood, and headed to the tent on the left.

"Mom." She stood. The minute Romeo followed suit, the green and indigo flames in the brazier snuffed out.

"I'm tired, Lily. And all the talking is... That's all." She waved at them without turning and stepped through the flap.

The werewolf draped his arm around Lily's shoulders and pulled her closer. "Did that go the way you thought it would?"

"Yes and no." She let her head fall sideways against his chest and sighed. "I bet once I get some real sleep for the first time in...I don't know how long, I'll be able to think better."

He squeezed her a little closer against him. "Do you mind if I join you?"

"You don't ever have to ask me that again."

They moved toward the other tent, and the thought of a huge bed and twelve to fourteen hours of uninterrupted sleep almost made her collapse before they reached the entrance. *I probably won't get a full eight, but anything's better than nothing. I would know.* She reached for the tent's flap, but he caught her wrist gently and lowered her arm.

"Hold on a second."

"What—"

He took her face in both hands and kissed her. When she breathed in, all the tension she'd carried for months seeped to her toes and into the weirdly purple clover beneath her bare feet. He pulled away and pressed his forehead against hers. "You know what we really are, though, right?"

With her eyes still closed, she smiled. "What's that?"

"Whatever we wanna be."

THIRTY

In Paris, France, Gabriel Mercier stepped into his office, shut the door behind him and leaned against it, and closed his eyes. *A moment's peace would be nice. Is that too much to ask?*

He took a deep breath and rolled out the kink in his shoulders. Half an hour. That was all he had before his meeting with the owner of a bed and breakfast in the southern part of the city who called at least three times a day, swearing she'd seen another werewolf casting spells at the top of the Eiffel Tower.

"Or a witch who turns into a wolf. Either way, it's the same, isn't it?" He shook his head and opened his eyes. "Huh. Hello."

Resting in the center of his office was a stone a little larger than a golf ball. It pulsed with a shimmering golden light and emitted enough magical energy on its own to tell him it was considerably more worthy of his attention—and his time—than Madame Ateur's spellcasting werewolf sightings. There was no note beside the stone and no other discerning features, and he hadn't missed a phone call or a text all day.

The witch detective for Paris' Non-Magical Relations department locked his office door and let the strap of his shoulder bag slide off his arm. The bag met the floor with a thump, but he didn't take his gaze off the glowing stone for a second.

"This is exactly what I don't need to deal with today." He stepped toward it and ran a hand over the day-old stubble on his cheeks. Squinting, he circled the anonymously sent gift—hopefully—but couldn't make head or tails of it. He lowered into a squat and peered a little closer. When he reached out tentatively until his finger was only a few inches away, the stone vibrated there on his twenty-year-old carpet. "That's interesting..."

A sharp buzz from his back pocket startled him back to reality. Answering phones and documenting complaints was, in fact, eighty percent of his job. Or it should have been and hadn't been for the last few months. Not since multiple someones had chosen to fling magic around under the public eye without a care for the consequences.

With another frown at the stone, Gabriel removed his cell phone from his back pocket and stood. He didn't take his gaze off the odd package on his office floor as he answered the call and put the phone to his ear. "Mercier."

"Mr. Mercier. My name in Bentley McClure."

"American." He raised his eyebrows and effortlessly switched his side of the conversation into English. "I don't get many calls from the US of A, Monsieur McClure."

"Be that as it may, this phone call is particularly important. A young witch named Lily Antony gave me your number with very clear instructions as to the nature of my communication with you. We need to talk."

"And why is that, if you please?"

The man on the other end of the line cleared his throat. "I understand you may have heard of an organization calling themselves the Black Heron Society."

Gabriel finally turned away from the stone and stepped past his desk toward the window. He slipped a few fingers through the shade and pulled it aside to study the street five stories below. "Please continue, Monsieur McClure. You have my full attention."

Lily, Romeo and Greta have escaped The Black Heron Society, but just barely. They now need to get help to put an end to what Carmichael is planning. Join them in the final battle in Homeward Witch.

Get sneak peeks, exclusive giveaways, behind the scenes content, and more.
PLUS you'll be notified of special **one day only fan pricing** on new releases.

Sign up today to get free stories.

CLICK HERE

or visit: https://marthacarr.com/read-free-stories/

For Hire: Teachers for special school in Virginia countryside.

Must be able to handle teenagers with special abilities.

Cannot be afraid to discipline werewolves, wizards, elves and other assorted hormonal teens.

Apply at the School of Necessary Magic.

AVAILABLE AT AMAZON RETAILERS

Austin robbery detective Maggie Parker knows how to run down a felon. Now add in magic.

When she finds a gnome breaking into her garage to steal a favorite wooden puzzle box everything changes. Did she just see a compass fly?

Can she learn how to use the magic of bubbles to chart a new course in time? It's a lot harder than it sounds.

Join her on her quest to rescue passengers on an ancient ship – a big blue marble called Earth – and save herself.

<u>AVAILABLE ON AMAZON AND IN KINDLE UNLIMITED!</u>

It's the end of a year and a decade, for me as well as the calendar. I turned 60 last September and frankly, I'm really looking forward to what this last chapter has to offer.

For most of my days I've had a very competitive spirit. That's got good and bad aspects to it. Good side – willing to work hard and be creative to get ahead. Bad side – don't always appreciate where I am and sometimes I forget to ask, what do I want?

But, turning 60 has me asking that a lot. Not only that question, but instead of wondering if someday I'll finally lose enough weight, I think, what if you don't? Are you going to hate who you are from here to the end of the story? Suddenly, that seems ridiculous. I wish that thought had occurred to me thirty years ago, but I'm grateful I'm getting it now. I have the usual short list of maybe some days and as each one pops up, there's that new thought. It's changing everything.

I've bought more clothes that fit this size and when I

pass by mirrors, I've been looking for things to love instead of examining what I wish would go away. Exercise has been narrowed down to what I like, instead of what makes me look good to others. I dropped the classes I hated and I'm sticking with yoga and swimming, with some run/walking mixed in. Spin class or circuit training fills me with dread.

I've also swung all of my writing projects under the LMBPN umbrella. It's resulted in the new Terranavis Universe and a lot more assistance from the LMBPN machine. I've found it's more fun to work with others, plus less work for me. Win, win. All of those books start coming out in late December.

I've been trying meditation more lately and find I have a better day on the mornings I fit it in. It's said that meditation is when you learn to listen. Kind of fits with the whole vibe I have going on and goes along with being less competitive.

It's gotten easier to cheer others on without wondering how I can get in the race with them. Or look at someone's fabulous travel pics on Facebook and remember how much I like being in my dream house or over at the amenity center. (It's a grownups playground over there).

Plus, this holiday season I got back to baking and made hundreds of gingerbread men and women for the first time. They turned out great! My piping left something to be desired but, hey, taste is really what matters.

I bagged up a half dozen to a clear bag with candy canes on them, put red rope and a card with my house number, name and phone number on each one, and went up and down my street and tied one to a door. It worked like a charm! I've gotten texts and met more of my neighbors and now, we have each other's phone numbers. I think throwing a cocktail party for my neighbors, grown up and old school style (dressed up, no kids, real hors d'oeuvres) is in my future.

I'm looking forward to the next decade being more balanced, peaceful and full of fun. I'm already finding writing to be more fun, less stress as I work on new Leira books and finish a big fantasy book with Michael that will be out soon. It's all adding up to a more balanced life – just what I wished for at the beginning of 2019 and a great way to enter the next phase. May you each see your dreams fulfilled with joy, peace and ease. More adventures to follow.

OTHER BOOKS BY MARTHA CARR

Series in the Oriceran Universe:

SCHOOL OF NECESSARY MAGIC
SCHOOL OF NECESSARY MAGIC: RAINE
CAMPBELL
ALISON BROWNSTONE
THE DANIEL CODEX SERIES
THE LEIRA CHRONICLES
I FEAR NO EVIL
FEDERAL AGENTS OF MAGIC
THE UNBELIEVABLE MR. BROWNSTONE
REWRITING JUSTICE
THE KACY CHRONICLES
MIDWEST MAGIC CHRONICLES
SOUL STONE MAGE
THE FAIRHAVEN CHRONICLES

Other series:

THE LAST VAMPIRE
THE WITCH NEXT DOOR

OTHER BOOKS BY JUDITH BERENS

OTHER BOOKS BY MARTHA CARR

**JOIN THE ORICERAN UNIVERSE FAN
GROUP ON FACEBOOK!**

CONNECT WITH THE AUTHORS

Martha Carr Social

Website: http://www.marthacarr.com

Facebook: https://www.facebook.com/
groups/MarthaCarrFans/

Michael Anderle Social

Michael Anderle Social
Website:
http://www.lmbpn.com

Email List:
http://lmbpn.com/email/

Facebook Here: https://www.
facebook.com/TheKurtherianGambitBooks/